Bryn looked up at Gabriel ...ply. 'I don't see how, when w. appearance are so ... years ago.'

...her had awake...
...ue the eighteen-year-o...
...illed her night-time fantasies
...her father's arrest, and months
...that had ended.

...same fantasies had filled all of her nights
...ce meeting Gabriel again a week ago. The
...ame desire had caused her breath to catch in
her throat when she turned to look at him. This
man—Gabriel—awakened that hunger inside
her just by being in the same room with her.

THE DEVILISH D'ANGELOS

Sinners named for saints…

Known around the world for the prestigious
Archangel auction houses and galleries, in London,
New York and Paris, the D'Angelo brothers are
notorious for their prowess in the art world…and even
more so for their exploits in their personal lives.

These Italian heartthrobs might have been named
for angels, but their ruthless natures and powerful
personas make them *anything* but angelic…

Soar to LONDON for *Gabriel D'Angelo's* story in:
A BARGAIN WITH THE ENEMY
February 2014

Sail to NEW YORK for *Raphael D'Angelo's* story in:
A PRIZE BEYOND JEWELS
April 2014

And coming soon…
Fly to PARIS for *Michael D'Angelo's* story in:
A D'ANGELO LIKE NO OTHER
March 2014

Enter the exclusive world of the D'Angelos
in this dazzling new trilogy from
Carole Mortimer!

A BARGAIN
WITH THE ENEMY

BY
CAROLE MORTIMER

Published in Great Britain 2014
by Mills & Boon, an imprint of Harlequin (UK) Limited,
Eton House, 18-24 Paradise Road, Richmond, Surrey, TW9 1SR

© 2014 Carole Mortimer

ISBN: 978 0 263 90821 3

Harlequin (UK) Limited's policy is to use papers that are natural,
renewable and recyclable products and made from wood grown in
sustainable forests. The logging and manufacturing processes conform
to the legal environmental regulations of the country of origin.

Printed and bound in Spain
by Blackprint CPI, Barcelona

Carole Mortimer was born in England, the youngest of three children. She began writing in 1978, and has now written over one hundred and fifty books for Harlequin Mills & Boon®. Carole has six sons: Matthew, Joshua, Timothy, Michael, David and Peter. She says, 'I'm happily married to Peter senior; we're best friends as well as lovers, which is probably the best recipe for a successful relationship. We live in a lovely part of England.'

Recent titles by the same author:

Did you know these are also available as eBooks?
Visit www.millsandboon.co.uk

To my six wonderful sons. I am so proud of you all.

PROLOGUE

'DON'T WORRY, MIK, he'll be here.'

'Take your damned feet off the desk,' Michael snapped in reply to his brother's reassurance, not even glancing up from the papers he was currently reading in the study at Archangel's Rest, the secluded Berkshire home of the D'Angelo family. 'And I'm not worried.'

'Like hell you're not!' Rafe drawled lazily, making no effort to swing his black-booted feet down from where they rested on the front of his older brother's desk.

'I'm really not, Rafe,' Michael assured mildly.

'Do you know if—?'

'I'm sure it can't have escaped your notice that I'm trying to read!' Michael sighed his impatience as he glared across the desk. He was dressed formally, as usual, in a pale blue shirt and neatly knotted navy blue silk tie, dark waistcoat and tailored trousers, the jacket to his suit draped over the back of his leather chair.

It had always been something of a family joke that their mother had chosen to name her three sons Michael, Raphael and Gabriel to go with the surname D'Angelo, and the three brothers had certainly taken their fair share of teasing about it when they were at boarding school. Not so much now they were all in their thirties, and the three of them had been able to utilise their names by making the three Archangel auction houses and galleries in London, New York and Paris the most prestigious privately owned galleries in the world.

Their grandfather, Carlo D'Angelo, had managed to bring his wealth with him when he fled Italy and settled in England almost seventy years ago before marrying an English girl, and producing a son, Giorgio: Michael, Raphael and Gabriel's father.

Like his father before him, Giorgio had been an astute businessman, opening the first Archangel auction house and gallery in London thirty years ago, and adding to the D'Angelo wealth. When Giorgio retired ten years ago and he and his wife Ellen settled permanently in their Florida home, their three sons had turned that comfortable wealth into a veritable fortune by opening up similar Archangel galleries in New York and Paris, resulting in them now all being millionaires many times over.

'And don't call me Mik,' Michael instructed harshly as he continued to read from the file in front of him. 'You know how much I hate it.'

Of course Rafe knew that, and he considered it part of his job description as a younger brother to annoy the hell out of his older sibling!

Not that he had as many opportunities to do that nowadays with the three brothers usually at a different gallery at any one time. But they always made a point of meeting up for Christmas and each of their birthdays, and today was Michael's thirty-fifth birthday. Rafe was a year younger and Gabriel, the 'baby' of the family, another year younger at thirty-three.

'I last spoke to Gabriel a week or so ago.' Rafe made a face.

'Why the grimace?' Michael quirked a dark brow.

'No reason in particular—we all know that Gabe's

been in a bad mood for the past five years. I never understood the attraction myself.' He shrugged. 'She looked a mousy little thing to me, with just those big—'

'Rafe!' Michael cautioned in a growl.

'—grey eyes to recommend her,' Rafe completed dryly.

Michael's mouth thinned. 'I spoke to Gabriel two days ago.'

'And?' Rafe prompted impatiently when it became obvious his older brother was doing his usual clam impersonation.

Michael shrugged. 'And he said he would arrive here in time for dinner this evening.'

'Why the hell couldn't you have just told me that earlier?'

Rafe swung his booted feet impatiently down onto the carpeted floor before rising restlessly to his feet. He ran an irritated hand through the short thickness of his sable-dark hair as he paced the room, tall and leanly muscled in a fitted black T-shirt and faded denims. 'That would have been too easy, I suppose.' He paused his pacing to glower at his older brother.

'No doubt.' Michael gave the ghost of a smile, eyes dark and unreadable, also as usual.

The three brothers had similar colouring, height and build; all a couple inches over six feet tall, with the same sable-black hair. Michael kept his hair short, his eyes so dark a brown they gleamed black and unfathomable.

Rafe's hair was long enough to curl down onto his shoulders, his eyes so pale a brown they glowed a deep gold.

'Well?' he rasped impatiently as Michael added nothing to his earlier statement.

'Well, what?' His brother arched an arrogant brow as he relaxed back in his leather chair.

'How was he?'

Michael shrugged. 'As you said, as bad tempered as ever.'

Rafe grimaced. 'You two are the pot and the kettle!'

'I'm not bad tempered, Rafe, I just don't choose to suffer fools gladly.'

He raised dark brows. 'I trust I wasn't included in that sweeping statement…?'

'Hardly.' Michael relaxed slightly. 'And I prefer to think of all three of us as perhaps being just a little… intense.'

Some of Rafe's own tension eased as he gave a rueful grin in acknowledgement of the probable reason none of them had ever married. The women they met were more often than not attracted to that dangerous edge so prevalent in the D'Angelo men, as much as they were to their obvious wealth. Obviously not a basis for a relationship other than the purely—or not so purely!—physical.

'Maybe,' he conceded dryly. 'So what's in the file you've been looking at so intently since I arrived?'

'Ah.' Michael grimaced.

Rafe eyed him warily. 'Why do I have the feeling I'm not going to like this…?'

'Probably because you aren't.' His brother turned the file around and pushed it across the desk.

Rafe read the name at the top of the file. 'And who might Bryn Jones be?'

'One of the entrants for the New Artists Exhibition being held at the London gallery next month,' Michael supplied tersely.

'Damn it, that's the reason you knew Gabriel would be back today!' He glared at his brother. 'I'd totally forgotten that Gabriel's taking over from you in London during the organisation of the exhibition.'

'And I get to go to Paris for a while, yes,' Michael drawled with satisfaction.

'Intending to see the beautiful Lisette while you're there?' He eyed his brother knowingly.

Michael's mouth tightened. 'Who?'

The dismissive tone of his brother's voice was enough to tell Rafe that Michael's relationship with the 'beautiful Lisette' was not only over, but already forgotten. 'So what's so special about this Bryn Jones that you have a security file on him?'

Rafe knew there had to be a reason for Michael's interest in this particular artist. There had been dozens of eager applicants for the New Artists Exhibition; since Gabriel had organised the first one in Paris three months ago and it had been such a success, they had decided to go ahead and hold a similar one in London next month.

'Bryn Jones is a she,' Michael corrected dryly.

Rafe's brows rose. 'I see....'

'Somehow I doubt that,' his brother drawled dismissively. 'Maybe this picture will help....' Michael lifted the top sheet of paper to pull out a black and white photograph. 'I had Security download the image from one of the security discs at Archangel yesterday—' which explained the slightly grainy quality of the picture '—when she came into the gallery to personally deliver her portfolio to Eric Sanders.' Eric was their in-house art expert at the London gallery.

Rafe picked up the photograph so that he could take a closer look at the young woman pictured coming through the glass doors into the marbled entrance hall of the London gallery.

She was probably in her early to mid-twenties. The

black-and-white photograph made it difficult to tell her exact colouring. Her just-below-ear-length hair, in a perky flicked-up style, looked to be light in shade, her appearance businesslike in a dark jacket and knee-length skirt, with a pale blouse beneath the jacket—none of which detracted in the least from the curvaceous body beneath!

She had a hauntingly beautiful face, Rafe acknowledged as he continued to study the photograph: heart-shaped, eyes light in colour, pert little nose between high cheekbones, her lips full and poutingly sensual with a delicately pointed chin above the slenderness of her throat.

A very arresting, and slightly familiar, face.

'Why do I have the feeling that I know her?' Rafe asked, lifting his head.

'Probably because you do. We all do,' Michael added tersely. 'Try imagining her slightly more…rounded, with heavy, black-framed glasses, and long mousy-brown hair.'

'Doesn't sound like the sort of woman any of us would ever be attracted to—' Rafe broke off abruptly, his gaze narrowing sharply, suspiciously, on the black-and-white photograph in front of him.

'Oh, yes…. I forgot to mention that perhaps you should look closely at…the eyes,' Michael drawled dryly.

Rafe glanced up quickly. 'It can't be! Can it?' He studied the photograph more closely. 'Are you saying this beautiful woman is Sabryna Harper?'

'Yes,' Michael bit out crisply.

'William Harper's daughter?'

'The same.' Michael nodded grimly.

Rafe's jaw tightened as he easily recalled the uproar five years ago when William Harper had offered a supposedly previously unknown Turner for sale at their London gallery. Ordinarily the painting would have remained a secret until after authentication had been made and confirmed by the experts, but somehow its existence had been leaked to the press, sending the art world and the media into an excited frenzy as speculation about the painting's authenticity became rife.

Gabriel had been in charge of the London gallery at the time, had gone to the Harper family home several times to discuss the painting while it was being authenticated, meeting both the wife and daughter of William Harper on those occasions. This made it doubly difficult for him when he'd had to declare the painting, having undergone extensive examination by the experts they had brought in from all over the world, to be a near-perfect forgery. Worse than that, the police investigation had proved that William Harper was solely responsible for the forgery, resulting in the other man being arrested and sent to prison for his crime.

His wife and teenage daughter had been hounded by the media throughout the trial and the whole sorry story had blown up again when Harper had died in prison just four months later, after which his wife and daughter had simply disappeared.

Until now, it would seem....

Rafe eyed Michael warily. 'Are you absolutely sure it's her?'

'The file you're looking at is from the private investigator I hired after I saw her at the gallery yesterday—'

'You *spoke* to her?'

Michael shook his head. 'I was passing through the entrance hall when Eric walked by with her. As I said, I thought I recognised her, and the private investigator was able to establish that Mary Harper resumed using her maiden name just weeks after her husband's death, and her daughter's surname was changed to the same by deed poll.'

'And this Bryn Jones is really her?'

'Yes.'

'And what do you intend doing about it?'

'Doing about what?'

Rafe breathed his impatience with his brother's continued calm. 'Well, she obviously can't be one of the six new artists exhibited at Archangel next month.'

Michael raised dark brows. 'Why can't she?'

'Well, for one thing her father was put in prison for attempting to involve one of our galleries in selling a forged painting!' He eyed his brother. 'Not only that, but Gabriel went to court and helped to put him there!'

'And the sins of the father are to be passed down onto the daughter, is that it?'

'No, of course that isn't it! But—with a father like that, how do you even know the paintings in her portfolio are her own?'

'They are.' Michael nodded. 'It's all in the file. She attained a first-class arts degree. Has been trying to sell her paintings to other galleries for the past two years with very little success. I've looked at her portfolio, Rafe, and, despite what those other galleries may have thought, she's good. More than good, she's original, which is probably why the other galleries refused to take a chance on her work. Their loss is our gain. So much so that I have every intention of buying a Bryn Jones painting for my own collection.'

'She's going to be one of the final six artists?'

'Without a doubt.'

'And what about Gabriel?'

'What about him?'

'We warned him repeatedly but he refused to listen. She's the reason he's been in a bad mood for five years—how do you think he's going to feel when he realises exactly who Bryn Jones really is?' Rafe bit out exasperatedly.

'Well, I think you'll agree, she's definitely improved with age!' Michael said dryly.

There was no doubt about that. 'This is just— Damn it, Michael!'

Michael's mouth firmed. 'Bryn Jones is a very talented artist, and she deserves her chance of being exhibited at Archangel.'

'Have you even stopped to think *why* she might be doing this?' Rafe frowned. 'That she might have some ulterior motive, maybe some sort of revenge plot against us or Gabriel for what happened to her father?'

'It did occur to me, yes.' Michael nodded calmly.

'And?'

He shrugged. 'I'm willing to give her the benefit of the doubt at this stage.'

'And Gabriel?'

'Has assured me on numerous occasions that he's an adult, and certainly doesn't need his big brother interfering in his life, thank you very much!' Michael drawled dryly.

Rafe gave an exasperated shake of his head as he began pacing the study. 'You seriously don't intend to tell Gabriel who she is?'

'As I said, not at this stage,' Michael confirmed. 'Do you?'

Rafe had no idea yet what he was going to do with this information....

CHAPTER ONE

One week later...

SHE WAS ENTERING the enemy camp—again!—Bryn realised with a frown as she paused outside on the pavement to look up at the marble frontispiece of the biggest and the best of the privately owned galleries and auction houses in London, the name Archangel in large gold italics glittering in the sunlight above the wide glass entrance doors. Doors that swung open automatically as she stepped forward before walking purposefully into the high-ceilinged entrance hall.

Purposefully, because this really was the enemy camp as far as Bryn was concerned. The D'Angelos, Gabriel in particular, had been responsible for both breaking her heart and sending her father to prison five years ago....

She couldn't think of that now, couldn't allow herself to think of that now. She had to focus on the fact that the past two years of rejection from gallery after gallery were what had brought her to this desperate moment. The same two years, after leaving university with her degree, when she had believed the world was now her oyster, only to learn that the recognition she craved for her paintings was ever elusive.

Many of her friends from university had caved to the

pressure of family and stretched finances and entered advertising or teaching instead of following their real dream of painting for a living. But not Bryn. Oh, no, she had stuck doggedly to her desire to have her paintings exhibited in a London gallery, believing that one day she would be able to make her mother proud of her and erase the shame of her family's past.

Two years later she had been forced to admit defeat, not by abandoning her paintings, but by being left with no choice but to enter the New Artists competition at Archangel.

'Miss Jones?'

She turned to look enquiringly at one of the two receptionists sitting behind the elegant cream-and-rose marble desk, which was an exact match for the rest of the marbled entrance hall; several huge columns in the same marble stretched from floor to ceiling, with beautiful glass cabinets protecting the priceless artefacts and magnificent jewellery on display.

And this was only the entrance hall; Bryn knew from her previous visit to the Archangel Gallery that the six salons leading off this vast hallway all housed yet more unique and beautiful treasures, and there were many more being prepared for auction in the vast basement beneath the building.

She straightened, determined not to be intimidated—or at least not to *reveal* that she was intimidated—by her elegant surroundings, or by the cool blonde and elegant receptionist who couldn't be much older than her own twenty-three years. 'Yes, I'm Miss Jones.'

'Linda,' the other woman supplied as she stood up from behind the desk and walked across the entrance hall, the three-inch heels of her black shoes clicking on the marble floor as she joined a hesitant Bryn still standing near the doorway.

Bryn felt distinctly underdressed in the fitted black trousers and loose flowered silk shirt she had chosen to wear for her second meeting with Eric Sanders, the gallery's in-house art expert. 'I have an appointment with Mr Sanders,' she supplied softly.

Linda nodded. 'If you would care to follow me to the lift? Mr D'Angelo left instructions for me to take you upstairs to his office as soon as you arrived.'

Bryn instantly stiffened, her feet suddenly feeling so leaden they appeared to have become weighted to the marble floor. 'My appointment is with Mr Sanders.'

Linda turned with a swish of that perfectly groomed blonde hair as she realised Bryn wasn't following her. 'Mr D'Angelo is conducting the interviews this morning.'

Bryn's tongue felt as if it were stuck to the roof of her suddenly dry mouth. 'Mr D'Angelo?' she managed to squeak.

The older woman nodded. 'One of the three brothers who own this gallery.' Bryn knew exactly who the three D'Angelo brothers were. She just had no idea which one Linda was referring to when she said 'Mr D'Angelo'. The haughty and cold Michael? The arrogant playboy Raphael? Or the cruel Gabriel, who had taken her naive heart and trampled all over it?

It didn't really matter which of the D'Angelo brothers it was; they were all arrogant and ruthless as far as Bryn was concerned, and she wouldn't have come within twenty feet of a single one of them if not for the fact that she was as determined to become one of the six artists chosen to take part in the Archangel New Artists Exhibition next month, as she was desperate.

She gave a slow shake of her head. 'I think there's

been some sort of mistake.' She frowned. 'Mr Sanders' secretary phoned me and made the appointment.'

'Because Mr D'Angelo was out of the country at the time,' Linda said, nodding.

Bryn could only stand and stare at the other woman, wondering if it was too late for her to just cut and run while she still had the chance....

Gabriel rested his elbows on his desktop as he watched the link to the security camera in the entrance hall of the gallery on his laptop.

He had recognised Bryn Jones the moment she entered the gallery, of course. Seen the way she hesitated, before her expression turned to one of confusion as Linda spoke to her, followed by total stillness as her face went completely blank, making it easy for Gabriel to guess the moment Linda had told her that her appointment this morning was now with him rather than Eric.

Bryn Jones...

Or, more accurately, Sabryna Harper.

The last time Gabriel had seen Sabryna had been five years ago, day after day across a crowded courtroom. She had glared her dislike of him with glittering but velvet-soft dove-grey eyes from behind dark-framed glasses every time she so much as glanced at him. And she had glanced at him a lot!

Sabryna Harper had only been eighteen at the time, her figure voluptuously rounded, her manner a little clumsy and self-conscious, light brown hair growing silky and straight to just below her shoulders, dark-framed glasses making her eyes appear large and vulnerable. A vulnerability and appeal that Gabriel had been inexplicably drawn to.

Her figure had slimmed down to a svelte elegance that

was shown to full advantage in a loose floral blouse and fitted trousers. The light brown hair looked as if it had been given blonde highlights, as well as being expertly cut and styled as it winged out perkily about her ears, nape and creamy, smooth brow. And she had dispensed with the dark-framed glasses, probably in favour of contact lenses. She also possessed a new self-confidence that had allowed her to walk into Archangel with purpose and determination.

The loss of weight was even more noticeable in her face; there were now slight hollows in her cheeks, revealing sculptured cheekbones either side of a pert little nose. Her mouth— Thank God Rafe had warned him about that sexy mouth. As it was, he had an arousal that would need several minutes to subside—the same minutes it would take Linda to bring Bryn Jones to his office, he hoped.

Would Gabriel have recognised this beautiful and confident young woman as the Sabryna Harper of five years ago if Rafe hadn't prewarned him of her real identity, after Michael had decided to act with his usual arrogance by remaining silent on the subject?

Oh, yes, Gabriel had no doubts he would have recognised Sabryna. Voluptuous or slender, glasses or no glasses, slightly gauche or elegantly poised, he would have known Sabryna under any guise she cared to take on.

The question was, would she betray by word or deed that she remembered him too?

Delicious, decadent, sinful, melted-chocolate brown. It was the only way to describe the colour of Gabriel D'Angelo's eyes, Bryn acknowledged with self-disgust as, Linda having delivered her to his office, she now stood in front of the marble desk looking at the man she had long considered her nemesis. The man who, with the whiplash of his arrogant and ruthless tongue, had not only helped to send her father to prison, but also succeeded in killing Sabryna Harper and necessitating that Bryn Jones rise from her ashes.

The same man that the youthful Sabryna had been beguiled by, kissed by and lost her heart to five years ago.

The same man who only weeks later had stood in a courtroom and condemned her father to prison.

The same man that Sabryna had looked at across that courtroom and known that she still wanted, despite what he was doing to her father. Just looking at him had aroused her when she should have felt nothing but hatred for him, robbing her of both breath and speech.

A reaction, a dangerous attraction, that in the years that followed Bryn had convinced herself she hadn't felt. That the emotions that had bombarded her whenever she looked at him must have been dislike, perhaps even hate, because she couldn't have still been attracted to him after what he had done to her family.

One look at him now and Bryn knew that she had been lying to herself for all these years; that Gabriel D'Angelo, despite being the one man she should never have been attracted to, never have allowed herself to be flattered by or allowed to kiss her, had then, and still now, held a dangerous fascination for her.

So much so that she could feel how his overpowering presence managed to dominate the dramatic and opulent elegance of the huge office with floor-to-ceiling windows looking out over the London skyline and original artwork adorning all of the delicate pink-silk-covered walls.

Gabriel D'Angelo…

A man who should by now—Bryn had many times

wished it so!—be balding, running to fat, with lines of dissipation etched into his overbloated and self-indulgent face.

Instead, he was still well over six feet of taut, lean muscle, all shown to advantage in a dark and tailored designer-label suit that probably cost as much as a year of Bryn's university fees! And his hair was just as thick and dark as she remembered it too, brushed casually back from his face to fall in silky ebony waves to just below the collar of his cream silk shirt.

As for his face…!

It was the face of a male model. The sort of face that women of all ages would have drooled over before buying whatever it was he was selling; a high intelligent brow above those sinful brown eyes, his nose aquiline, cheekbones high and sharply defined against light olive skin—with not a line in sight, of dissipation or otherwise! He had perfect chiselled lips—the top one fuller than the bottom—and the strong line of his jaw was exactly as Bryn remembered it: square and ruthlessly determined.

'Miss Jones.' His cultured voice, as Bryn had discovered five years ago, wasn't in the least accented, as might have been expected from his name, but was as English as her own. The same deep and husky rumble of a voice that had once caused Bryn's knees to quake, and had still done so even as she had listened to that voice condemn her father and seal his fate.

Bryn almost took a step back as Gabriel D'Angelo stood up and moved out from behind the marble desk. She managed to stand her ground as she realised he had only risen to his feet in order to hold out his hand to her in greeting. A lean and elegant hand totally in keeping with the strength Bryn could discern in every leanly muscled inch of him.

The sort of strength that she had no doubts was capable of crushing every bone in her own much smaller hand, if he chose to exert it.

Bryn gave an inward jolt as she realised he was studying her just as closely through narrowed lids, those melted chocolate-brown eyes appearing to see everything and miss nothing.

Would he recognise her as Sabryna Harper? Somehow she doubted it, given the fact that the gauche Sabryna, despite Gabriel having kissed her once, would have made very little impact on the life of a man like Gabriel D'Angelo, and there would have been so many other women in his life—and his bed!—during the past five years.

Besides which, her name was different, and she looked dramatically different: she was twenty pounds lighter, her hair was now cut short with blonde highlights, her face thinner, more angled, and she wore contact lenses rather than dark-framed glasses.

But was it possible—could Gabriel D'Angelo have recognised her, despite those changes?

Bryn moved one sweat-dampened hand surreptitiously against the thigh of her trousers before raising it with the intention of brushing it as briefly as possible against his much larger hand. A move Gabriel D'Angelo instantly circumvented as those long, lean fingers closed firmly about, and retained hold, of Bryn's—instantly renewing and deepening that jolt of electricity, the sexual awareness, as it throbbed from his hand into hers, moving the length of her arm before settling in the fullness of her breasts, causing her nipples to tingle and harden beneath her blouse.

A jolt that Gabriel D'Angelo also felt, if the tightening

of his fingers about hers and the increased narrowing of those captivating eyes, was any indication.

'We meet at last, Miss Jones,' Gabriel murmured as he deliberately continued to hold the slenderness of her hand firmly within his own.

Bryn blinked, her expression suddenly wary, those dove-grey eyes even more beautiful now that they weren't hidden behind glasses. 'I—I'm not sure what you mean.'

Gabriel wasn't completely sure what he meant either!

Rafe's advice, when the two brothers had met for dinner before he flew back to New York five days ago, had been that the easiest and best way for Gabriel to avoid any further unpleasantness with the Harper family was to simply tell Eric Sanders to take Bryn Jones off the list of possible candidates for the upcoming New Artists Exhibition.

And on a professional level Gabriel understood exactly why his brother had given him that advice; given the circumstances of his past history with her late father William Harper, it was sound, even necessary, advice.

Except…

Gabriel had a history with Bryn too. Brief, admittedly, just a stolen kiss when he had driven her home from visiting Archangel one evening, but he had hoped for more at the time, had thought of Bryn often the past five years, had wondered, speculated, what would have become of the two of them if not for the scandal that had ripped them apart.

Gabriel wasn't in the least proud of the part he had played in the events of five years ago. Not William Harper's conviction and incarceration for fraud, his death in prison just months later or the way in which his wife and teenage daughter had been hounded and harassed during the whole ordeal.

Against his brother's advice Gabriel had tried to see Sabryna, both during the trial and after her father was sent to prison, but she had turned him away every time, refusing to answer the door to him and changing her number so he couldn't call her either. Gabriel had decided to step back, to give her time, before approaching her again. And then William Harper had died in prison, putting an end to any hopes Gabriel might have had for himself and Sabryna ever having a relationship.

He had also taken an objective look, a purely professional look, over the past few days at the paintings Bryn Jones had submitted to the competition. They were really good—her still-life paintings so delicately executed it was almost possible for him to smell the rose petals falling gently down from the vase. To want to reach out and touch the ethereal beauty in a woman's eyes as she looked down at the baby she held in her arms.

Gabriel could see genuine talent in every brush stroke, the sort of rare artistic talent that would one day make Bryn Jones' paintings highly collectable, as both objects of beauty as well as a sound investment. Because of this Gabriel didn't feel he could eliminate her as a candidate for the New Artists Exhibition just to save himself from the discomfort of facing her and having her hate every breath of air he took.

He did, however, have every intention of keeping the question of Bryn Jones' own motivation for entering the competition in the forefront of any of his future dealings with her.

Gabriel released her hand abruptly before moving to retake his seat behind the desk, very aware that his earlier arousal had returned with a vengeance the moment he had touched the silky softness of Bryn's hand. 'I was referring to the fact that you're the seventh, and last, can-

didate to have been interviewed in the past two days.'
The only candidate that Gabriel was interviewing personally, but she didn't need to know that.

Her cheeks slowly paled. 'The *seventh* candidate?'

He gave a dismissive shrug. 'It's always best to have a reserve, don't you think?'

She was a *reserve*?

Bryn had been so desperate she had swallowed her pride, her dislike of all things D'Angelo, to enter their damned competition, only to be told she was a reserve?

Bryn had thought—*believed*—that being asked to come in to Archangel for another interview meant that she had been chosen as one of the final six artists for the Archangel New Artists Exhibition. And now Gabriel D'Angelo was telling her she was a reserve! Like an actor who was expected to learn all the lines and then stand in the wings of the theatre every night, in the full knowledge they might never have the chance to appear on the stage!

Had she been recognised after all? And if she had, was this Gabriel D'Angelo's idea of amusing himself, of extracting further retribution for the scandal her father had brought upon the Archangel Gallery, and the three brothers who owned it, five years ago?

'Are you quite well, Miss Jones?' A frown now creased Gabriel's brow as he stood up once again and moved round the desk. 'You've gone very pale....'

No, Bryn wasn't 'well'. In fact she was feeling far from well! So much so that she didn't even attempt to back away as Gabriel moved far too close to her. She had swallowed her pride, risked everything, the whole persona and life she had made for herself these past five years, by even bringing herself to the attention of the

D'Angelo brothers, only to now be told she wasn't good enough!

'I— Is it possible I could have a glass of water?' She raised a slightly shaking hand up to the dampness of her brow.

'Of course.' Gabriel was still frowning darkly as he strode across to the bar.

She was a reserve.

How disappointing was that?

How humiliating was that?

Damn it, she had been living in a state of nervous tension since entering the competition and this was the thanks she got at the end of all that anxiety, all that swallowed pride: to be made the reserve artist for the Exhibition!

'I've changed my mind about the water,' she snapped tautly as she straightened. 'Do you have any whisky in there?'

Gabriel turned slowly, eyes narrowing as he saw that colour had returned to Bryn Jones' cheeks, her eyes taking on a similar angry glow. A glow he easily recognised as being the same one he had felt directed at him across the courtroom. Why was Bryn suddenly so angry? They had been in the middle of a conversation about—

Ah. Gabriel had stated she was the seventh candidate being interviewed in a six-candidate competition.

Gabriel strolled back with the glass of whisky she had asked for. 'I believe there's been a misunderstanding—'

'There certainly has.' She nodded, taking the crystal glass of whisky he held out to her and drinking it down in one swallow, only to breathe in with a gasp before coughing as the fiery alcohol hit the back of her throat.

'I think you'll find that thirty-year-old single-malt whisky is meant to be sipped and savoured rather than guzzled down like lemonade at a child's birthday party,' Gabriel drawled dryly as he took the empty glass from her slightly lax fingers and placed it safely on his desk as she bent over at the waist, obviously still fighting for breath. 'Should I—?'

'Do not even think about slapping me on the back!' she warned through gritted teeth as she straightened and saw his raised hand, her cheeks now a fiery red, eyes ringed with unshed tears caused by her choking fit.

At least, Gabriel hoped they were caused by her choking fit and not from disappointment. She had obviously misunderstood his earlier comment; he had caused this woman enough heartache already in her young life. 'Would you care for that glass of water now...?'

She glared even more fiercely. 'I'll be fine,' she snapped. 'As for your offer, Mr D'Angelo—'

'Gabriel.'

She blinked long silky lashes. 'I beg your pardon?'

'I asked that you call me Gabriel,' he invited warmly.

A frown settled on her face. 'What possible reason could I have for wanting to do that?'

Gabriel eyed her mockingly; with her hair styled in that short spiky fashion, at the moment she looked very much like a bristly, indignant hedgehog! 'I thought, perhaps, in the interest of...a friendlier working relationship?'

She gave an inelegant snort. 'We have no relationship, Mr D'Angelo, friendly, working or otherwise.' She picked up her shoulder bag from where it had fallen to the floor during her choking fit. 'And, while I'm sure many artists would feel flattered to be chosen seventh out of a six-candidate competition, I'm afraid I'm not one of them.' She turned sharply on her heel and marched towards the door.

'Bryn.'

She came to an abrupt halt at hearing her name spoken in that throaty rumble through those perfectly sculptured lips. The same chiselled lips that had once kissed her, that had filled her fantasies every night for months before, during, and after her father's trial and incarceration.

Her name sounded…sensual, when spoken in that husky voice. Soft, seductive and definitely sensual. A sensuality Bryn's body instantly responded to, her breasts once again feeling fuller, the nipples firming, aching.

Bryn turned slowly, her expression wary as she acknowledged, inwardly at least, that her traitorous body still thought Gabriel D'Angelo was the most decadent, wickedly attractive man she had ever set eyes on.

And it shouldn't.

She shouldn't.

How could she possibly still feel this way when this man had been instrumental in destroying her family?

They had been five tough years for both Bryn and her mother. The two of them had remained living in London while her father was in prison, only changing their surname and moving out of London after he had died.

On top of their grief had come the ordeal of finding somewhere to live, finally moving into the cottage they had found to rent in a little Welsh village.

Then had come the difficulty of Bryn finding and getting into a university that allowed her to live at home; she hadn't wanted to leave her still-devastated mother on her own. Her mother was a trained nurse, and had found a job at a local hospital, but Bryn had had to settle for working in a local café and fitting her hours of study around her work shifts.

In amongst all that change and struggle there hadn't been a lot of time for men in Bryn's life—the odd date here and there, but never anything prolonged or intimate. Besides which, any serious involvement would have eventually necessitated that she confide her real name wasn't Bryn Jones at all, and that her father had been William Harper, something she had been loath to do.

At least Bryn had thought, until now, that was the reason she had avoided any serious involvement....

To look at Gabriel D'Angelo now, however, to hear his voice again, and realise that *he* was the reason behind her lack of interest in other men, was humiliating in the extreme.

To realise, to know, that it was this man's sensual good looks, that deep voice, that filled her senses and created a sexual tension within her without even trying.

To acknowledge that the hateful Gabriel D'Angelo, a man who had kissed her just the once, a kiss he had no doubt regretted as soon as it had happened, had been the yardstick against which Bryn had judged all other men for the past five years, was not only masochistic madness on her part, but disloyal to both her mother, and her father's memory....

CHAPTER TWO

'YOU'VE GONE PALE again,' Gabriel said, striding determinedly towards where Bryn now stood transfixed and unmoving by the closed door of his office. A dark scowl creased his brow as he saw how the colour had once again leeched from those creamily smooth cheeks. 'Perhaps you should sit down for a minute—'

'Please don't!' She stepped back and away from the hand Gabriel had raised with the intention of lightly grasping her arm, her fingers tightly clutching her bag, her eyes deep pools of dark and angry velvet-grey as she gave a determined shake of her head. 'I have to go.'

Gabriel's mouth tightened at her aversion to his even touching her. 'We haven't finished our discussion yet, Bryn—'

'Oh, it's definitely finished, Mr D'Angelo,' she assured him spiritedly. 'As I said, thank you for the—the honour, of being chosen as the seventh candidate, but I really have no interest, or time, to waste on being a runner-up.' Her eyes flashed darkly. 'And I have no idea why you would ever have thought that I—'

'You were far and away the best of the six candidates to be chosen for the exhibition, Bryn,' Gabriel bit out briskly—before she had chance to dig a bigger hole for herself by insulting him even further. 'I saved the best till last,' he added dryly.

'That I might be, so thank you for your interest, but—' She broke off her tirade to stare up at him blankly as his words finally trickled through the haze of her anger. She moistened her lips—those sexily pouting lips!—with the tip of her tongue before speaking again. 'Did you just say...?'

'I did,' Gabriel confirmed grimly.

'But earlier you said— You told me that I was the seventh person being interviewed—'

'And one of the previous six is the reserve. And happy to be so,' he added harshly.

Bryn stared up at Gabriel as the full horror of what she had just done, what she had said, was replayed back to her in stark detail. At the same time realising he was right; at no time had Gabriel said she was the seventh-place candidate, only that she was the seventh artist being interviewed.

She swallowed as the nausea washed over her, and then swallowed again, to absolutely no avail, the single-malt whisky she had 'guzzled down like lemonade at a child's birthday party' obviously at war with her empty stomach; she had been far too tense about coming back to the gallery to be able to eat any breakfast this morning. 'I think I'm going to be sick!' she gasped as she raised a hand over her mouth.

'The bathroom is this way,' Gabriel said quickly, lightly grasping her arm and pulling her towards a closed door on the opposite side of the office.

Bryn didn't fight his hold on her this time, too busy trying to control the nausea to bother resisting as he threw open the bathroom door and pushed her inside. Bathroom? It was more like something you would find in a private home, with a full glass-enclosed walk-in shower along one wall, along with the cream porcelain facilities, and had to be as big as the whole of the bedsit in which Bryn had lived and painted this past year!

Bryn dropped her bag to the floor and ran across the room to hang her head over the toilet only just in time, as she immediately lost her battle with the nausea and was violently and disgustingly sick.

'Well, that really was a complete waste of a thirty-year-old single-malt whisky!' Gabriel commented dryly some minutes later, when it became obvious from Bryn's dry retching that she had nothing else left in her stomach to bring up.

Adding further to her humiliation Bryn realised he must have remained in the bathroom the whole time she was being physically ill. 'I'll buy you a replacement bottle,' she muttered as she flushed the toilet, and avoided so much as glancing at the dark figure looming in the doorway as she moved to the sink to turn on one of the gold taps and splash cold water onto her clammy cheeks.

'At a thousand pounds a bottle?'

Bryn's eyes were round with shock as she lowered the towel she had been patting against her cheeks, before turning to look at him as he leaned against the doorframe, arms folded across the broad width of his muscled chest.

She instantly wished she hadn't looked at him as mockery gleamed evidently in his eyes. 'Who pays that sort of money for—? You do, obviously,' she acknowledged heavily as he raised his dark brows. 'Okay, so maybe I can't afford to buy you a replacement bottle right now.'

He gave an appreciative and throaty chuckle. And instantly threw Bryn into a state of rapid, heart-thumping awareness.

It had been years since she had seen Gabriel laugh—there had been no room for humour or soft words between them once her father had been arrested!—and the transformation that laughter made to his harshly handsome face reminded her of exactly why she had fallen so hard for him all those years ago.

She had believed—hoped—that if they should ever meet by chance, she wouldn't still respond to him like this, but the warmth that now shone in his eyes, the laughter lines beside those eyes and the grooves that had appeared in his chiselled cheeks, along with the flash of straight white teeth between those sculptured and deeply sensual lips, instantly proved how wrong she had been to hope. Gabriel might be sinfully handsome when he wasn't smiling, but he became lethally so when he was!

Bryn abruptly averted her gaze to finish drying her face and hands before checking her appearance in the mirror behind the sink—dark shadows beneath tired eyes, pale cheeks, throat slender and vulnerable. A vulnerability she simply couldn't afford in this man's presence.

She took a deep, controlling breath before turning back to face Gabriel. 'I apologise for my comments earlier, Mr D'Angelo. They were both rude and premature—'

'Stop there, Bryn,' he interrupted as he straightened. 'Abject apology doesn't sit well on your defensive shoulders,' he explained as she looked at him warily.

Angry colour rushed back into her cheeks. 'You could have at least let me finish my apology before mocking me.'

He was obviously having difficulty holding back another smile as he answered her. 'As I just said, abject apology doesn't appear to come naturally to you!'

She sighed at the deserved rebuke. 'I apologise once again.' Bryn didn't even attempt to meet his mocking gaze now as she instead kept her gaze fixed on the beautiful marble floor. She might know exactly why she harboured such resentment against this man, but as she had guessed—hoped—Gabriel didn't remember her at all, and she didn't want to do or say anything that would make him do so either.

'Shall we go and finish our conversation now?' he prompted briskly. 'Or do you need to hang over my toilet for a while longer?'

Bryn gave a pained frown. 'It was the whisky on top of an empty stomach.' And the fact that she knew, as did he, that she had prejudged his words without so much as a single hesitation!

'Of course it was,' Gabriel humoured dryly as he stood aside for Bryn to precede him back into the office, only too well aware that it was her resentment towards him for past deeds that was responsible for her having jumped to the wrong conclusions. 'And it's sacrilege to drink single-malt whisky any other way but neat.'

'At that price I can see that it would be, yes,' he heard Bryn mutter derisively. A mutter he chose to ignore as he instead returned to the reason for her being there in the first place. 'As I said, you are definitely one of the six candidates to have been chosen for the New Artists Exhibition being held in the gallery next month. Shall we sit down and discuss the details?' He indicated the comfortable brown leather sofa and chairs arranged about the coffee table in front of those floor-to-ceiling picture windows.

'Of course.' She noticeably chose to sit in one of the

armchairs, rather than on the sofa, before crossing one of her knees neatly over the other and looking up at him questioningly.

Gabriel didn't join her immediately, but went to the bar instead to take a bottle of water from the refrigerator, collecting a clean glass as well, then walking back to place them both down on the coffee table in front of her before lowering his length down into the chair opposite hers.

'Thank you,' she murmured softly, taking the top off the bottle and pouring the water into the glass. She took a long, grateful swallow before speaking again. 'Mr Sanders told me some of the details last week but obviously I'm interested in knowing more…' Her tone was businesslike.

Gabriel studied her through narrowed lids as they went on to discuss the details of the exhibition more fully, Bryn writing down the details in a notebook she had taken from her bulky shoulder bag.

Five years ago this woman had still been sweetly innocent, a young woman poised on the cusp of womanhood, a combination that had both intrigued and fascinated him. The passing of those years had stripped away all that innocence, in regard to people and events, at least; Gabriel had no way of knowing whether Bryn was still physically innocent, although somehow he doubted it. Five years was a long time.

But not only had Bryn grown more beautiful during those years, she had also grown in confidence, especially where her art was concerned, and she talked on the subject with great knowledge and appreciation.

'Have you ever thought of working in a gallery like Archangel?' Gabriel prompted as their conversation drew to an end half an hour later.

Bryn looked up from placing her notebook back into her handbag. 'Sorry?'

He shrugged. 'You're obviously knowledgeable on the subject, enthusiastic and bright, and those things would make you an asset to any gallery, not just Archangel.'

Bryn frowned as she looked warily at Gabriel across the glass coffee table, not sure if she had understood him correctly. 'Are you offering me a job?' she finally prompted incredulously.

He returned her gaze unblinkingly. 'And if I was?'

'Then my answer would have to be no! Thank you,' she added belatedly as she realised she was once again being rude, a rudeness that was totally out of keeping with her expected role as one of the grateful finalists in the New Artists Exhibition.

'Why would it?'

'Why?' She gave an impatient shake of her head at his even having to ask that question. 'Because I want my paintings to hang in a gallery, to hopefully be sold in a gallery, not to work as an assistant in one!'

He shrugged. 'Do you have something against taking a job to help pay the bills until that happens?'

Bryn eyed him guardedly, only too aware that her rent was due to be paid next week and that she had other bills that had reached the red-reminder stage too. And yes, a job did help to pay the bills, but she already had a job, at yet another café, even if it didn't pay nearly well enough to cover both her monthly rent and the bills, no matter how much she tried to economise.

It was almost as if Gabriel had guessed that and was offering her charity....

She instantly chided herself; of course Gabriel D'Angelo wasn't trying to help her. He just knew, as she did, that she was more than capable of doing the job he was offering, and he had no doubt assumed she would jump at the chance to work at Archangel, based on the fact that, historically, artists were known for starving in garrets.

Bryn wasn't starving, exactly, she just didn't eat some days. And while her third-floor bedsit wasn't exactly a garret, it was barely big enough to swing the proverbial cat in, with one half of the room put aside for sleeping and cooking and the other half utilised as her studio.

'No, of course not,' she answered him lightly. 'But I already have a job—'

'At another gallery?'

Bryn frowned as she heard the sharpness in his tone. 'What does it matter where I work?'

He raised dark brows. 'It matters in this case because it would hardly be appropriate for your paintings to be displayed at Archangel when you're working for another gallery.'

Good point, Bryn acknowledged ruefully. 'Right.' She nodded. 'Well, I don't work for another gallery. But I do have a job,' she continued briskly as she bent down to retrieve her bag from the floor. 'And my next shift starts in half an hour, so—'

'Your next…shift?'

'Yes, my next shift,' Bryn confirmed abruptly, stung by the incredulity in his cultured voice. 'I work behind the counter in a well-known coffee-shop franchise.'

His brows rose. 'Latte, cappuccino, espresso and a low-calorie muffin? That sort of coffee-shop franchise?'

The previous half an hour of conversation had gone smoothly; it had even been enjoyable at times, as they'd discussed which paintings from her portfolio Bryn was going to show at the exhibition next month, the timelines and other necessary details. But that had so obviously only been a brief lull in the tension between them if Gabriel had now decided to pull his arrogant-millionaire rank on her. Bryn eyed him challengingly. 'You have something against coffee shops?'

Those sculptured lips thinned. 'I don't recall ever having been inside one.'

Of course he hadn't; people as rich as Gabriel D'Angelo frequented exclusive restaurants and fashionable bars, not high-street coffee shops.

'But I do have something against one of my artists working in one of them, yes,' he continued evenly.

She stiffened. 'One of your artists?'

'This will be your first public exhibition, I believe?' he prompted evenly.

'I've sold one or two paintings in smaller galleries in the past couple years,' she came back with defensively.

'But am I right in thinking this will be the first time that so many Bryn Jones paintings have been shown together in an official exhibition?'

'Yes…' Bryn confirmed slowly.

He nodded. 'Then in future, whether you like it or not, your name will be linked with the Archangel Gallery.'

Bryn certainly didn't like it. It had felt as if she were being forced to walk over burning-hot coals by even entering her paintings in a competition being run by the hateful D'Angelo brothers; she certainly didn't like the idea of her name being for ever linked with either them or their galleries.

She hadn't even told her mother of the desperation that had forced her to enter the competition, dreaded thinking how her mother would react if she were to ever find out Bryn was having her work shown at *this* gallery!

And maybe Bryn should have thought about that a

little more deeply before deciding to walk over those burning hot coals and enter the competition.

Gabriel could almost actually see the war being waged inside Bryn's head. The natural desire to have her artistic talent not only shown for the first time but also recognised for the talent that it was, obviously totally at war with her desire not to be in the least beholden, or associated with in the future, either the D'Angelo name or the Archangel Gallery. Yet another indication of how much she still disliked him and all he stood for. If he had needed any. Which he didn't.

'Your point being?' Bryn now prompted guardedly.

He grimaced. 'I think it would look better in the catalogue being printed and sent out to our clients before the exhibition if you weren't listed as currently working in a coffee shop.'

'Better for whom?'

Gabriel bit back his irritation with her challenging tone, having no intention of admitting that he had already known about her working in a coffee shop—and that it was him, personally, who didn't like the idea of her working there. He might never have been into such an establishment, but he had driven past them numerous times, and the thought of Bryn being run ragged in such an establishment, day after day—evening after evening— just so that she could pay her bills every month, wasn't particularly appealing.

Besides which, Gabriel also knew, from the discreet enquiries he had made about her once Rafe had told him exactly who she was, that Bryn Jones suffered a constant struggle to pay those bills. A job as an assistant at Archangel would go a long way to relieving her of that burden, at least.

A dark frown creased his brow. 'What possible rea-

son could you have for refusing a job here if it was offered to you?'

'Let me see...' She lifted a finger to her chin in exag-
gerated thought. 'First, I don't want to work in a gallery.
Second, I don't want to work in a gallery. And third, I
don't want to work in a gallery!' Her eyes glittered determinedly.

'This gallery in particular, or just any gallery?' Gabriel questioned evenly.

'Any gallery,' Bryn answered firmly. 'Besides,
couldn't it be considered as a little...incestuous, if I were
to start working at Archangel now?' she forestalled Gabriel D'Angelo's next comment lightly.

'Because of your inclusion in the exhibition?'

'Exactly,' she confirmed with satisfaction.

His mouth tightened. 'And that's your final answer?'

'It is.'

He scowled darkly. 'You're very...intractable in your
attitude, Miss Jones.'

'I prefer to think of it as maintaining my independence, Mr D'Angelo,' Bryn came back sharply.

'Perhaps,' he drawled as he stood up in one fluid
movement, the dryness of his tone implying he thought
the opposite. 'I think we've said all that needs to be said
for today. I have another appointment in—' he glanced
at the expensive-looking gold watch on his wrist '—ten
minutes or so.' He looked at her expectantly as she remained seated.

'Oh. Right.' Bryn stood up so hastily she accidentally
kicked her bag across the floor, instantly scattering the
contents far and wide. 'Hells bells and blast it!' She immediately dropped to her knees on the carpeted floor,
her cheeks flushing with embarrassment as she began
collecting up her scattered belongings, some of which

were personal in the extreme, and cramming them back into her handbag.

'I've always wondered what women kept in their hand-bags,' Gabriel D'Angelo drawled in amusement.

'Well, now you know!' Bryn had paused to glare up at him, and instantly became aware of how his well over six feet of lean muscle towered over her so ominously. 'And I would get this done a whole lot quicker if you were to help rather than just stand there grinning!' Like an idiot, she could have added, but didn't, because it wouldn't have been the truth.

The last thing Gabriel was, or looked like when he grinned in that way, was an idiot; devilishly rakish, dev-astatingly attractive—lazily, sensuously so—and maybe even boyishly mischievous, as that grin knocked years off his age, but he certainly didn't look like an idiot.

Besides which he had stopped grinning now, those chocolate-brown eyes narrowed on her in totally male assessment.

A frown creased Gabriel's brow as he looked down at Bryn on her hands and knees in front of him. It was a… provocative pose, to say the least. As the ever-increasing bulge in his trousers testified.

Bryn's cheeks were flushed, her lips slightly moist and parted and it should be illegal what those black trousers did for her heart-shaped bottom—and Gabri-el's arousal—bent over like that…!

'Right,' he rasped harshly as he crouched down beside her, his gaze averted as he gathered up the notebook and pen she had been using to make notes in earlier, as well as a small bottle of hand cream and a lip salve. 'Hell's bells and blast it…?' he prompted gruffly, aware of her perfume now; nothing so anaemic as something floral for Bryn Jones, she was a mixture of spices, with an underlying hint of sensual woman.

He saw her shrug out of the corner of his eye. 'My mother has never approved of a woman swearing, so I learnt to improvise at an early age.'

Gabriel only half listened to her answer as he moved down onto his knees. The smell of those spices—cinnamon, something fruity, maybe a hint of honey and that more elusive smell of sensual woman—all served to increase his awareness of the woman beside him. 'A pot of white pepper, Bryn?' he questioned as he held it up for inspection.

'It's cheaper than pepper spray!' She snatched the pot from his hand before thrusting it back into her bag.

Gabriel sat back on his heels to look at her. 'Pepper spray?'

'I have to walk home late at night several times a week.' She dismissed his concern without looking up, missing the frown of disapproval that clouded Gabriel's face.

'From the coffee shop,' he said stiffly.

She gave him a brief glance before looking away again. 'Why does that bother you so much?'

Good question. But not one Gabriel could answer. Not without revealing that he knew exactly who she was, and the part he felt he had played in her current circumstances—something her defensive attitude told him she definitely didn't want from him.

And the past half hour in Bryn Jones' company was enough to tell him that what she claimed as independence was actually defensive pride, and that she had more than her fair share of it.

Because of the scandal involving her father five years

ago? No doubt that was a contributing factor, but Gabriel had a feeling she would have always been more than a little prickly; her feistiness was all too apparent in those flashing eyes and the stubborn tilt of her pointed chin.

'I thought you had another appointment in a few minutes?' She gave Gabriel a pointed look as he knelt unmoving beside her.

Make that a whole lot prickly! 'I was just wondering what a third party, if they should walk into my office right now, would make of the two of us being down here on the floor together like this,' Gabriel came back with deliberate and husky provocation.

'We may just find out if your next appointment arrives early!' Colour warmed her cheeks as she bent over to retrieve a lipstick from beneath the coffee table.

As that next appointment was the elderly Lord David Simmons, an avid art collector, Gabriel worried the other man might have a heart attack on the spot if he should catch so much as a glimpse of Bryn's shapely backside!

'Did I say something amusing?' Bryn sat back on her heels to look at Gabriel, who was grinning again, his dark hair having fallen rakishly over his forehead, causing Bryn's hands to curl into fists as she resisted the impulse to touch those silky dark locks.

'Private joke.' His grin faded, his eyes deepening almost to black as he continued to look at her intently.

Except Gabriel wasn't looking at all of her, Bryn realised self-consciously, just her lips. Moist and slightly parted lips that she immediately clamped shut as she rose abruptly to her feet and slung her bag over her shoulder.

Only to as quickly freeze in place as she realised, with their difference in height, that Gabriel's face was now level with her breasts.

A fact he took full advantage of as he made no effort to hide his interest in the fact that he could see Bryn's bared breasts beneath the gauzy material of her floral blouse....

CHAPTER THREE

'Mr D'Angelo…?'

'Hmm?' Gabriel couldn't look up from the mesmerising view he currently had of Bryn's breasts, full and perfect breasts, tipped by rosy areolas and plump nipples. Rapidly firming nipples that deepened in colour even as he continued to gaze at them.

'Mr D'Angelo? Gabriel!' Bryn's voice became more urgent as he failed to respond.

Gabriel ran the tip of his tongue moistly over his lips as he imagined taking those nipples into his mouth and suckling hungrily, his roused shaft instantly throbbing its approval of the idea. 'You aren't wearing a bra….'

'No. I—'

'Do you intend to wear this blouse to work today?' He scowled at the thought of Bryn's seminaked breasts being ogled by other men across the counter of a high-street coffee shop.

'We're all required to wear a black T-shirt with the franchise logo on it,' Bryn answered him dismissively. 'And will you please get up!' She grasped hold of his arm and tried to pull him to his feet.

A move that jiggled those plumped and roused breasts temptingly in front of Gabriel's heated gaze. If he just moved forward, ever so slightly, he would be able to put his mouth on them and actually taste—

'Damn it, Gabriel, someone is knocking on the door!' Bryn hissed. The urgency of her tone, as much as the words, finally broke through Gabriel's sexual haze, causing him to frown darkly as he realised exactly what he was doing. What he had been thinking of doing.

And with whom....

Bryn breathed out shakily as Gabriel finally rose abruptly to his feet, running his fingers impatiently through his hair as he shot her a scowling glance before striding across the room to wrench open the outer door.

'I'm sorry, Mr D'Angelo, I didn't realise Miss Jones was still here.' The receptionist took a wary step back as she obviously saw and recognised the aggression in Gabriel's scowling expression.

'Good to see you again, Gabriel!' The elderly man at the receptionist's side appeared less concerned as he greeted the younger man warmly before stepping into the room and giving Bryn a friendly if curious glance. 'Are you going to introduce me to your young lady?' he prompted Gabriel.

'I'm just Mr D'Angelo's previous appointment,' Bryn supplied quickly, dismissing even the suggestion of her and the arrogant Gabriel D'Angelo ever being a couple. 'And I've already taken up far too much of his time,' she added lightly as she joined them near the open doorway before turning a cool gaze on the still-frowning Gabriel.

Damn it, she was doing her best to allay the speculation she had seen in the receptionist's eyes and the curiosity in Gabriel's visitor's. The least Gabriel could do was try to reciprocate rather than continuing to scowl his irritation at the interruption!

An interruption of what? Bryn wondered....

There had been no doubting the hunger she had seen in those seductive eyes as Gabriel had looked at her breasts so appreciatively, or the flush of arousal high in those sculptured cheeks as he had begun to lean towards her. Evidence that, if they hadn't been interrupted by the knock on the door, he would have acted on that unmistakable hunger, and actually kissed her breasts? Perhaps more than kissed them?

Bryn felt her knees go weak just thinking of having those sculptured lips latching on to her aroused nipple, suckling deeply, his tongue a hot and arousing rasp—

'Bryn, this is Lord David Simmons.' Gabriel's voice was harsh as he made the introduction. 'David, this is Bryn Jones.' His tone softened to politeness. 'One of the six artists whose paintings will be appearing in the New Artists Exhibition next month.'

'Indeed?' David Simmons' warm blue eyes lit up with pleasure as he and Bryn shook hands. 'I'm very much looking forward to attending the exhibition,' he informed Bryn warmly as he retained a hold on her hand. 'I flew over to Paris two months ago to attend the New Artists Exhibition at the Archangel Gallery there, and I can assure you you're in good hands with Gabriel here. He has a definite eye for recognising new talent.'

Bryn's smile froze on her lips, not just at being told she was in good hands with Gabriel but also because she knew, only too well, that Gabriel had a definite eye for spotting a forgery too. She released her hand from David Simmons'.

'Then no doubt I'll see you again next month, Lord Simmons—'

'Please, call me David,' he invited warmly.

'Bryn,' she returned tautly, very much aware of Gabriel's brooding presence beside her. 'Now, if you will all excuse me...? I have another appointment as well.'

Gabriel knew Bryn's other 'appointment' was her shift at the coffee shop, a fact that still displeased him greatly. His bad mood was added to by the way David Simmons, a man old enough to be Bryn's grandfather, had maintained far too long a hold of her hand when introduced.

'Linda, please make an appointment for Miss Jones, before she leaves, for her to see Eric on Monday,' Gabriel instructed abruptly.

'Certainly, Mr D'Angelo,' the receptionist responded brightly.

Bryn blinked her long lashes. 'May I ask what for?'

Gabriel's mouth tightened. 'We need more personal information and photographs for the catalogue we're sending out to existing clients—as I believe we discussed earlier?'

Her cheeks coloured slightly at the rebuke, and a flash of anger illuminated her eyes. 'Obviously I must have been so overwhelmed at being told I was one of the six artists chosen for the exhibition that I didn't hear all the details that followed.'

Some of Gabriel's tension eased as he saw the continued anger in Bryn's eyes accompany her too-sweetly-made statement. It also reminded him that Bryn had actually been physically ill, rather than 'overwhelmed', once he had fully explained her inclusion in the exhibition, a nausea she had no doubt still been suffering from when the two of them had sat down together and discussed the details of what still had to be done before the exhibition.

Not to mention the distracting attention he had given her breasts a few minutes ago!

Not that Gabriel was particularly proud of that lapse;

he had recognised five years ago that she represented a danger to his self-control, and his meeting today with the older and more self-assured—even more beautiful!— Bryn Jones had shown him that danger still existed. Very much so...

Perhaps he should have taken Rafe's advice after all and stayed well away from Bryn Jones.

'Just make the appointment, Bryn,' he bit out tersely. 'I'll instruct Eric that he needs to explain those details to you again on Monday.'

She turned to give the older man a warm smile. 'It was a pleasure to meet you, Lord Simmons. Mr D'Angelo.' Her voice had noticeably cooled, and there was no smile, or mention of her feeling any of that same pleasure in meeting Gabriel.

'Pretty girl,' David Simmons remarked as the two men watched Bryn join Linda out in the hallway before closing the door firmly behind her.

'Linda?' Gabriel deliberately misunderstood the older man.

David gave him a knowing glance. 'Does Miss Jones paint as beautifully as she looks?'

'More so, if anything,' Gabriel answered truthfully; Bryn's work really was exceptional, and he had no doubt that David Simmons would recognise that talent as easily as he had, and would most likely be happy to buy one of her paintings in the exhibition next month.

'Interesting...' The older man nodded as he followed Gabriel to the seating area in front of the window.

It wasn't until much later, after his business with David had been concluded and Linda had escorted the older man down the stairs that Gabriel was able to pause and replay his meeting with Bryn from earlier.

The prickly outspokenness she had been unable to

hide had shown that she hadn't even begun to forgive him for the part he had played in her father's downfall. A defensive manner that was also an indication of the resentment she felt at having to be even slightly beholden to the D'Angelo family—clearly telling Gabriel that Bryn wouldn't have entered the New Artists competition, or the Archangel Gallery, if she hadn't considered it the very last resort. It was—

A glance across the office showed something glinting from beneath one of the armchairs. A something that, upon closer inspection, proved to be an item that he knew must have fallen out of Bryn's handbag earlier.

'And what can I get you to drink this evening— Gabriel?' The last word came out much louder than Bryn would have wished after glancing up and seeing that her next customer was Gabriel D'Angelo.

A Gabriel D'Angelo who was much more casually dressed—but no less lethally attractive—than he had been in his office earlier today; he wore a thin black cashmere sweater, the sleeves pulled up to just below his elbows—which emphasised every toned muscle and dip of those broad shoulders, chest, and the flatness of his stomach—with faded denims resting comfortably on the leanness of his hips. His overlong dark hair had also been slightly tousled by the warm evening breeze outside and fell softly, rakishly, onto his brow.

He'd claimed earlier never to have been inside a coffee shop, which posed the question of what was he doing in one now? And not just any coffee shop, but the one in which Bryn worked, because there was no way she believed his being here was just a coincidence.

She frowned slightly as she realised the people in the queue behind Gabriel were getting restless; six o'clock in the evening was one of their busiest times, when the people leaving work called in to collect a drink and something to eat on their way home, or to linger in the coffee shop while they relaxed for an hour or so with friends. It was even busier as it was a Friday evening, and the end of the working week for most people.

'What can I get for you this evening, Mr D'Angelo?' she repeated tightly.

He looked up at the board behind her. 'Black coffee?'

'Black coffee,' she repeated slowly; the coffee shop served six different brands of coffee and just as many types, as well as several flavoured teas, all of which could have milk, runny or whipped cream or several different flavoured shots, and Gabriel was asking for black coffee!

He nodded. 'If it's not too much trouble,' he drawled derisively.

'It's no trouble at all.' Bryn was aware of the keen eyes of the manager fixed beadily on the two of them as she watched Bryn ring up the sale and take Gabriel's money—unless, of course, Sally was just enjoying the chance to ogle the six feet three inches of hot, heart-poundingly attractive man standing on the other side of the counter.

Which appeared to be what all the other women in the coffee shop were doing—surreptitiously by the ones with a man of their own, the others openly eating Gabriel up with their eyes!

'If you would like to follow me,' Bryn instructed sharply as she moved farther down the crowded counter to fill his order, at the same time allowing one of the other assistants to take her place and serve the next customer. 'What are you doing here, Mr D'Angelo?' she muttered under her breath as she prepared his tray.

'Sorry?'

'I said—'

'You'll have to speak up a little, Bryn,' he drawled. 'I can't hear you with all the other noise and chatter in the room.'

She shot him an irritated frown as she raised her voice slightly. 'I asked what you're doing here.'

'Oh.' He nodded. 'You left something of yours on my office floor when you left earlier today, and I thought you might want them back.'

Bryn stilled, her breath catching in her throat, as she realised that the half a dozen or so people standing closest to them had fallen silent as they overheard his remark, their eyes wide as they obviously drew their own conclusions as to what Bryn might possibly have left on Gabriel D'Angelo's office floor....

'Did you do that on purpose?'

Gabriel looked up at Bryn a short time later as she came over to wipe and clear the table next to the one where he sat in a comfortable armchair, enjoying his mug of surprisingly good Colombian coffee. 'Did I do what on purpose?'

She frowned, her skin appearing creamier than ever against the black T-shirt she now wore in place of the gauzy blouse of earlier. 'You implied— You deliberately gave the impression a few minutes ago that I had left an item of clothing on the floor of your office earlier today!'

He raised dark brows. 'I did?'

Bryn's mouth thinned as she pretended to wipe his table. 'You know you did.'

He had, yes. Because, until she had seen him, Bryn had looked relaxed and smiling as she served customers, that smile instantly replaced by an annoyed frown the moment she'd recognised him, arousing his own feelings of irritation.

It had been a mistake for him to come here at all; he accepted that now. He should have just passed her property on to Eric Sanders to give back to her on Monday, or bagged it up and had it delivered by courier to her tomorrow rather than come here personally.

He knew he should stay well away from Bryn, that it was better for both of them if he did so; she so obviously wanted nothing to do with him outside Archangel, and he knew from their meeting how dangerous she was to his self-control.

It seemed he just hadn't been able to stop himself from coming here when the opportunity presented itself.

His jaw tightened. 'I do have something of yours that I thought you might need returning to you sooner rather than later.'

'Really?' She eyed him sceptically.

Gabriel leaned back in the leather armchair to look up at her through narrowed lids. 'You know, Bryn, I've found your attitude towards me to be…less than polite since meeting you. Surprisingly so, considering that I'm one of the owners of the gallery where your paintings are going to be exhibited. If you have a problem with me, or my gallery, then perhaps now might be a good time for you to tell me what that problem is?'

A delicate blush coloured her cheeks as she chewed on her bottom lip, her artistic ambitions obviously once again at war with the past—and present—resentment Bryn felt towards him.

It was a resentment Gabriel understood, and sympathised with, but it rankled that Bryn still so obviously held him to blame for what had happened in the past; Gabriel wasn't responsible for William Harper's attempt to sell a forged Turner to the D'Angelos. Only for showing the other man up as the charlatan he so obviously was.

Bryn had initially talked herself into entering her paintings in the New Artists competition by reassuring herself that in all likelihood she would never have to meet any of the three D'Angelo brothers personally. She now found it totally disconcerting that she had met and spoken with one of them—twice in one day!—and that that one should happen be Gabriel!

Even so, she knew she deserved Gabriel's criticism. She *was* guilty of allowing the past to influence her manner towards him, something he must consider highly disrespectful, as well as puzzling, given that he only knew her as Bryn Jones, aspiring artist, and had given no indication of recognising her as Sabryna Harper. If Gabriel ever learned the truth, it would no doubt result in that seventh, reserve artist being asked to take her place in the exhibition!

'I apologise if I've seemed less than…grateful, Mr D'Angelo,' she muttered stiffly. 'Obviously it's a privilege and an honour to be chosen as one of the new artists to display their paintings in a gallery as prestigious as Archangel—'

'As I told you earlier, Bryn, abject apology doesn't sit well on your slender shoulders,' he drawled, dark eyes gleaming with mocking humour.

Her gaze fell from his. 'In that case, I believe you said you came here this evening to return something of mine?'

'I did, yes.'

'And?' she prompted.

He glanced down at the gold watch on his wrist. 'What time do you finish this evening?'

Bryn frowned. 'In a couple hours.'

'Eight o'clock?'

'Eight-fifteen,' she corrected warily.

He nodded. 'Then I'll meet you outside at eight-fifteen.'

Bryn's brows rose. 'I don't understand.'

He shrugged those broad shoulders. 'I think it would be a good idea for the two of us to have dinner together, so that we can discuss, and hopefully dispose of, whatever your problem is with me or my gallery.'

Bryn's mouth gaped open. Had she imagined it or had Gabriel just— Had he just invited her to have dinner with him tonight?

No, of course he hadn't, Bryn answered her own question; Gabriel had made a statement, not asked a question. Because he was a man used to issuing orders and then expecting them to be obeyed? Or simply because it didn't even occur to him that Bryn—or any other woman, for that matter—would ever think of turning down a dinner invitation with the darkly attractive and eminently eligible Gabriel D'Angelo?

Bryn had a feeling that both of those things were true, but going out to dinner with him, discussing whatever her problem was with him or his gallery, was *not* an option.

Gabriel could almost see the struggle going on inside Bryn's beautiful head as she tried to find a polite way of refusing his invitation.

An invitation Gabriel knew he never should have made when he couldn't even look at Bryn without wanting her and she so obviously detested the very sight of him.

This prickly Bryn was so different from the Sabryna of five years ago, but even then Gabriel had known how much her beauty and innocence had appealed to him. He had only kissed her the once, a sweet and yet arousing kiss, a kiss that had affected him so deeply he had continued to think about her for months after her father's trial was over and she had refused to so much as see Gabriel again, and off and on in the years that followed too, as he'd found himself wondering what she was doing with her life, if she was happy.

That single meeting with her earlier today had shown him that the woman she had become, the woman she was now, had just as deep an effect on him.

So much so that being alone in his office with her, knowing he would have been able to touch her soft and creamy skin if he had just lifted his hand, and that unique spicy, womanly smell of her had invaded his senses, had resulting in his thinking of nothing else but her for the past six hours.

As for his arousal…! That had been a pounding ache for those same six hours, and even now the hardness of his shaft was pressing painfully against the restricting material of his jeans.

Which was as good a reason as any for him to get the hell as far away from Bryn Jones as was possible.

'Obviously not,' he dismissed harshly, pushing his cooling mug of coffee away from him before standing up abruptly. 'These are yours, I believe,' he rasped abruptly as he withdrew a silver metal tube from the front pocket of his jeans.

Bryn was still so shocked by Gabriel's suggestion that the two of them have dinner together this evening that it took several seconds for her to register the significance of the metal tube he held out to her. 'My reading glasses…' she finally recognised softly as she took the tube from him, glancing up at him quickly—guiltily— as she realised he really had come here this evening to return something that had obviously fallen out of her handbag earlier.

She moistened her lips with the tip of her tongue before speaking. 'It was very kind of you to return them to me so promptly and in person.'

He gave a hard, derisive smile. 'That sounded as if it actually hurt.'

'Of course it didn't.' Her cheeks had warmed at the taunt. 'And I apologise if you think my manner towards you has been…less than polite. I really am grateful for the opportunity to show my paintings at Archangel.'

'As far as you're concerned, Bryn, I *am* the Archangel Gallery,' he admonished harshly.

And quite what she was going to do about that Bryn had no idea; she only knew, having come this far, having worked so hard and for so many years towards this, it was now totally unthinkable she should be forced to withdraw her paintings from the exhibition because of the man who owned and ran the gallery! Or for Gabriel to decide her manner was so unacceptable he decided to withdraw them for her.

'I'm not sure what you mean by that, Mr D'Angelo,' she prompted uncertainly; she hadn't forgotten those few brief moments of intimacy between them in his office earlier, when she had been certain that he was going to touch or kiss her breasts. But, grateful as she was that he hadn't recognised her, if Gabriel believed for one moment that his position as owner of the Archangel Gallery gave him some sort of power over her, then—

'I'm not sure I like your implication either, Bryn!' he responded, dismissing that illusion.

Her throat moved as she swallowed before speaking. 'Maybe we could go somewhere and grab a bite this evening after all? Talk this through—'

'I can see no point in us even attempting to do that unless you're going to be completely honest with me.' Those brown eyes glittered as he looked down the length of his nose at her. 'Are you going to be honest with me, Bryn?'

Bryn's breath caught in her throat as she looked up at him sharply, searchingly. Had Gabriel realised who she was after all?

Of course he hadn't! For one thing Bryn doubted this man had ever given so much as a single thought towards William Harper's wife and daughter once her father had been sent to prison. For another, she had changed so much in the past five years, not just her name, but the way she looked and behaved too that he couldn't possibly have recognised her as the gauche teenager he had once kissed. And last, if he had known who she really was, he would never have allowed her anywhere near him or his gallery—

'Bryn, I need you to go back on the counter now.' There was an underlying edge of steel to her manager's tone as her rebuke cut across the tension between Gabriel and Bryn.

Bryn gave a guilty start as she turned to face Sally, knowing that the pointed remark was deserved; she had been talking with Gabriel D'Angelo for far too long. 'I'll be right there,' she promised lightly before turning back to Gabriel. 'Shall I meet you outside at eight-fifteen?'

For a moment Gabriel thought about refusing, about walking away from this woman and not looking back.

The plans for the exhibition were well in hand, and as such there was absolutely no reason why the two of them should even meet again before the night of that exhibition. Eric was more than capable of handling any and all future meetings with Bryn Jones.

And there were far too many reasons why Gabriel should keep his distance from her....

CHAPTER FOUR

GABRIEL WAS STILL having second, third—and fourth!—thoughts as to the wisdom of meeting up with Bryn Jones again this evening as he sat in his parked car waiting for her to emerge from the coffee shop.

It didn't take too much intelligence to know what Bryn had been thinking earlier. Or to know why she had thought it. Gabriel's behaviour earlier hadn't exactly been businesslike, most especially that remark about her not wearing a bra. Especially considering the fact that he had been down on his knees in front of her, staring at her breasts, when he'd made it!

Which was, Gabriel had reasoned with himself, all the more reason for him to meet with her again this evening, if only to reassure her that the two of them were to have a business relationship in future and nothing more.

Gabriel's senses all went on full alert—making a complete nonsense of that last sentiment—as he looked through the smoked glass of the window beside him and saw Bryn step out of the coffee shop at last, a short denim jacket over top of the gauzy blouse she had worn earlier today, a frown darkening her creamy brow as she looked for him amongst the crush of people still milling about on the busy pavement.

No doubt she was adding tardiness, or standing her up completely, to Gabriel's already long list of sins.

'Bryn.'

She turned in the direction of Gabriel's voice, giving a rueful grimace as she saw he had emerged from the sleek black sports car parked illegally outside the coffee shop. The smoky black windows had prevented her from seeing him seated inside. 'Mr D'Angelo,' she greeted as she hurried over to where he stood. 'I hope I haven't kept you waiting long?' she murmured politely.

'Not in the least.' He just as politely opened the passenger door of the car before standing back to allow her to get inside. 'And it's Gabriel,' he reminded her gently.

Bryn didn't move, or respond to his comment. 'Er—there's a pizza place just round the corner.'

He grimaced. 'I saw it. And trust me, Bryn, what they serve isn't real Italian pizza.'

'But—'

'The name is D'Angelo, Bryn.' He quirked dark, pointed brows.

It hadn't been part of Bryn's plans for this evening to go off somewhere in Gabriel's car with him. She had envisaged them getting a quick slice at the place round the corner, an hour or so of—hopefully—pleasant conversation, before they each went their separate ways. But, considering this was supposed to be a conciliatory meeting, it would look petty for her to refuse him now—besides which, with his Italian ancestry he probably did know more about pizza than she did!

'Fine.' She gave a bright, unconcerned smile as she moved forward to slide into the black-leather passenger seat, determined that this evening was going to go better than their previous two meetings had. Determined that she was going to act more like the fledgling-artist-grateful-to-the-art-gallery-owner-for-this-opportunity that she was supposed to be.

She had to push firmly to the back of her mind that the sleek sports car, the interior smelling richly of leather, along with a spicy, totally male smell that was pure Gabriel, was so reminiscent of that evening he had kissed her.

Gabriel closed the passenger door once Bryn had settled into the seat, before moving back to the other side of the car and resuming his seat behind the wheel. 'You didn't have any trouble after I left earlier?' he prompted as he fastened his seat belt and turned on the ignition.

'No, it was fine,' she dismissed; there was no need to tell him of the lecture she had received from Sally earlier about not spending her time talking to one of the customers, no matter how hot he was, and how there were plenty of other people who would like her job if she didn't want it. 'Where are we going exactly?' Bryn prompted interestedly as Gabriel manoeuvred the vehicle out into the evening flow of traffic.

'It's a little family-run place I know in a back street in the East End— Trust me on this, Bryn,' he drawled as he noticed her surprise.

'I'm sure it's fine. I was just— It doesn't sound like your sort of place,' she amended awkwardly.

'My sort of place being...?'

Bryn realised she was once again on shaky ground as she heard the hard challenge in Gabriel's tone; it hadn't taken long for the tension to return between them, despite her earlier promise with herself to keep the conversation light and pleasant. 'I have absolutely no idea,' she answered honestly.

'Good answer, Bryn.' Gabriel chuckled wryly, his seat

all the way back to accommodate his long legs, and appearing very relaxed as his hands moved lightly on the steering wheel of the powerful sports car.

He had nice hands, Bryn noted abstractedly. Long and artistic, and yet gracefully powerful at the same time. 'How did you become such an art expert?' she prompted interestedly. 'Do you paint yourself? Or did you inherit the galleries?'

It was clear to Gabriel that Bryn had decided to make a concerted effort to be more polite to him and to keep their conversation impersonal rather than personal, if possible. Unfortunately she had chosen the wrong subject if that was her intention.

'I wanted to paint,' he answered abruptly. 'I even took a degree in art with that intention, only to very quickly realise that I'm someone who can appreciate art rather than be good enough to participate.'

'That's…unfortunate.'

'Very.' One of the biggest disappointments of Gabriel's life was realising that his real artistic talent was for the visual rather than painting itself.

Bryn was frowning slightly as she turned sideways in her seat to look at him. 'I can't imagine not being able to express myself through my painting.'

'The art world would be all the poorer for it too,' he assured gruffly. Knowing it was true, that Bryn showed an insight in her paintings, a sense, a knowing, for what was inside her subject, even a dying rose, rather than what was only visible with the naked eye; it was the quality that made her paintings so unique.

'The art world hasn't exactly been beating a path to my door before now,' she said with a shrug.

Gabriel gave her a sideways glance. 'That's probably because the galleries you've approached with your work

before now have all been looking for chocolate-box paintings, stuff they can sell to the tourists to hang in their
sitting rooms when they get back home to remind them
of their visit to London. Your paintings are too good for
that. Archangel would have no interest in showing them
if they weren't.'

Bryn had stilled beside him. 'I don't remember men-
tioning what galleries I've approached in the past.'

'You didn't need to,' Gabriel dismissed lightly, having
no intention of reigniting the tension between them by
confiding that he now had a file on her at Archangel—
another file on her. Michael apparently had one too, a
security file, although Gabriel hadn't seen that one. To be
fair, they now had a professional file on all seven of the
finalists of the competition, which listed previous sales,
of which Bryn had three. But Gabriel had good reason
to know that Bryn was more sensitive than most—quite
rightly so—about sharing the personal details of her life.

'But—'

'We're here,' Gabriel announced as he saw they had
reached Antonio's; just in the nick of time too, as Bryn
seemed intent on pursuing a subject he would rather not
continue. 'Don't be misled by the exterior. Or the interior either, for that matter,' he added dryly as he parked
the car in front of the small bistro before getting out and
moving around to open Bryn's door for her. 'Antonio
makes the best Italian food in London, and none of his
customers gives a damn about the decor.'

Bryn was glad of the warning as they walked into
the brightly lit interior. There was a strong smell of gar-
lic in the air, crowded tables covered with plastic red-
and-white-checked tablecloths, artificial plants dangling
from every conceivable nook and cranny and an overly
enthusiastic Italian tenor playing over the audio system.

'Toni sings and records all his own songs,' Gabriel explained as he saw Bryn wince at a particularly off-key moment.

'Something else I'm going to have to trust you on, hmm?' she came back teasingly. Only to stiffen as she realised what she had just said. And Gabriel D'Angelo was the very last man she should ever trust. For any reason.

'Gabrielo!' A round-faced and portly man rushed across the room to greet them, standing at least a foot shorter than Gabriel as he shook the younger man's hand enthusiastically. 'We 'ave not seen you 'ere for some time.'

'That's because I've been in Paris—'

'Aha, I see what has kept you away from us, Gabrielo.' Warm brown eyes had settled knowingly on Bryn. 'You 'ave brought your young lady to meet Mamma and me, yes?'

'No—' Bryn started to interrupt.

'I promised Bryn one of your famous pizzas with everything on, and a bottle of your best Chianti, Toni,' Gabriel interjected, cutting lightly across Bryn's denial as he took a firm hold of her elbow and squeezed warningly.

'No problem.' The older man beamed. 'You will find somewhere for you and your young lady to sit, and I will 'ave Mamma bring the wine to you.' He waddled off in the direction of the door at the back of the room marked Kitchen, stopping often to chat with one or other of his many customers.

Finding somewhere to sit wasn't as easy as it sounded; Gabriel was right, the place was heaving, despite the decor and the music. Luckily a young couple with a baby were just preparing to leave, and Bryn and Gabriel were able to grab their table before someone else did.

'This is wonderfully mad,' Bryn murmured a few

minutes later, feeling slightly bemused by all the people around them talking in loud voices, most of them in Italian, and gesticulating with their hands to emphasise a point.

Gabriel grinned. 'My mother always refers to Antonio's as "picturesque".'

Bryn looked across the table at him. 'Your mother comes here too?'

He nodded. 'My father insists on coming to eat here at least once a week whenever my parents are back in London.'

Bryn slipped off her jacket as she settled more comfortably on her chair. Talking about Gabriel's parents might not be ideal but it was certainly a safer subject than her own family. 'Where do your parents live?'

'They moved to Florida ten years ago when my father retired, and left the running of the original Archangel Gallery, which was all we had at the time, to myself and my two brothers.' Gabriel shrugged, surprising Bryn by appearing totally relaxed in his surroundings.

She smiled slightly. 'That would be Raphael and Michael.'

He grimaced. 'My mother's romantic choice of names rather than my father's.'

'And you've opened two more galleries since then, one in New York and one in Paris. With the Italian connection, why not Rome?'

'The D'Angelos have always visited Italy for pleasure, not work.' He gave one of those totally disarming smiles that made him appear several years younger and which made it all too easy for Bryn to guess exactly what sort of 'pleasure' the three D'Angelo brothers enjoyed when in Italy.

'Have you—?'

'Gabrielo!' A tall, voluptuous, dark-haired woman—no doubt Toni's wife—descended on them, placing a raffia-bottomed bottle of Chianti and two glasses down on the table before pulling a now-standing Gabriel in tightly against her overabundant bosom as she burst into a flourish of Italian.

'English, please, Maria.' Gabriel chuckled.

'You are as 'andsome as ever, I see!' She leant back to beam up at him. 'Ah, if I were only twenty years younger!' she added wistfully.

'Even if you were you would never leave Antonio.' Gabriel smiled at her warmly.

Bryn felt a bit disconcerted, both by the friendly way that Toni and Maria had greeted Gabriel, and his warm response to them in return. It was much easier for her to keep her own distance from Gabriel when she could continue to think of him as that cold and ruthless man who had sealed her father's fate. The warmth shown to him by Toni and Maria, and his own obvious and long-standing affection for both of them, revealed a completely different side to the arrogantly ruthless Gabriel D'Angelo than the one Bryn had come to expect. Especially following so quickly on the heels of those moments of intimacy between them in his office.

'Toni tells me you 'ave brought your young lady with you?' Maria eyed Bryn speculatively as she stepped away from Gabriel.

'No embarrassing Bryn, please, Maria!' Gabriel warned quickly as he slipped off his jacket and hung it on the back of his chair, wondering if it had been a wise move on his part to bring Bryn to Antonio's. The Italian couple were always asking when he intended settling down and having *bambinos*, and Bryn was the first woman he had ever brought here.

In his defence, bringing Bryn to Antonio's had been a knee-jerk reaction to her obvious belief that he was a man who thought himself far above frequenting high-street coffee shops, or little Italian bistros, instead favouring exclusive restaurants and bars. Gabriel had just forgotten to factor in the consequences of bringing a woman to Antonio's for the first time; in the past he had only ever come to the bistro with members of his family, knowing the women he usually dated wouldn't give a damn how good the food was—this little bistro simply wasn't fashionable enough or exclusive enough for their 'sophisticated' tastes.

Not that he thought Bryn unsophisticated. His sole reason for bringing her here had been to show her that he wasn't the arrogant sophisticate she so obviously believed him to be.

Nor should he think of this as being a date—

Oh, to hell with this; whatever his reason for bringing Bryn here, she was here now, and it was his own fault if he had to suffer Toni and Maria's teasing speculation. 'Maria, Bryn. Bryn, Toni's wife, Maria,' he introduced stiffly.

'None of this is what you expected, is it…?'

Bryn took a sip of the Chianti that Gabriel had poured into the two glasses, Maria having hurried off to the kitchen shortly after the introductions to see if their pizza was ready. Introductions where, Bryn had noted, Gabriel had made no effort to correct Maria's assumption as to who Bryn was—or wasn't!

And no, this disorganised and noisy bistro wasn't the sort of place Bryn would ever have imagined seeing the Gabriel D'Angelo she had met earlier at Archangel, when he had looked every inch a wealthy and arrogant D'Angelo brother in his designer-label suit and silk shirt and tie.

'I have every reason to hope the pizza will be as delicious as this Chianti,' she murmured noncommittally.

'Oh, it will be.' Gabriel nodded, dark eyes hooded as he looked across the table at her. 'But I probably should have taken you somewhere a little more…upmarket, to celebrate your inclusion in the New Artists Exhibition.'

Her brows rose. 'Then shouldn't the other five finalists, and the reserve, have been invited too?'

He gave a hard smile. 'No.'

'Oh.' Bryn could feel her cheeks warm, but wisely said nothing; she had already made one wrong assumption about Gabriel this evening, an assumption he had taken exception to, and she wasn't inclined to make another. 'Well, this is absolutely fine for me,' she continued quickly. 'I would probably have felt out of my depth somewhere overly sophisticated anyway. Dining out hasn't exactly been something I've done a lot of since— This is fine,' she repeated flatly, lowering her eyes to avoid meeting his suddenly piercing and probing gaze. She had almost—almost—said 'since my father went to prison'. A slip that could have been extremely costly to her inclusion in the exhibition.

Bryn had no doubts that it was the very informality of their surroundings that was responsible for her feeling so relaxed she had almost spoken without thinking, rather than the man seated opposite her. There was nothing about Gabriel that caused her to feel in the least relaxed—not his dangerous good looks, or her own unwelcome response to them.

'To you, Bryn.' Gabriel held up his glass in a toast, seeming unaware of her inner turmoil. 'Let's hope that the Archangel exhibition is not only a successful one but also the first of many for you.'

'I'll drink to that!' Bryn took a grateful sip of her own wine. 'Do you—? Oh, wow!' Her eyes widened as she saw Maria winding her way deftly through the other diners towards their table, holding aloft the biggest pizza Bryn had ever seen in her life. Maria placed the hot plate down in the centre of their table with the beaming instruction to 'Enjoy!' before she hurried off again.

Bryn's mouth watered as she stared down at the laden pizza, seeing pepperoni, mushrooms, onions, spinach, ham and aubergines.

'I hope you don't mind that there are no anchovies?' Gabriel shrugged ruefully. 'Toni knows that I don't like them.'

'Are you kidding? Who would ever miss them with all these other toppings?' Bryn laughed delightedly as she continued to look at the pizza.

Gabriel felt his mouth go dry as he drank in the sight of Bryn relaxed and smiling; those dove-grey eyes warm and glowing, her creamy cheeks slightly flushed, her full and sensual lips—that had no need of the lip gloss so many women wore and which Gabriel, for one, found such a turn-off—delectably plump and rosy.

And watching those tempting lips as Bryn ate the pizza was going to be nothing short of physical torture for him!

'Tuck in before it gets cold,' he encouraged gruffly. 'There are no knives and forks,' he added dryly as Bryn frowned slightly at the obvious omission of utensils from the table. 'The only way to eat pizza is with your fingers,' he explained as she looked up at him questioningly.

'Is that another Gabrielism?' she teased as she helped herself to a slice of the pizza.

'Trust me,' Gabriel murmured softly.

She stilled before raising suddenly guarded eyes. 'You keep saying that....'

Yes, he did. Because, after meeting Bryn again, after spending time with her this evening knowing that she believed he had no idea who she was, and knowing how much he still wanted her, Gabriel did want Bryn to trust him.

'I had a really good time this evening, thank you,' Bryn murmured as she and Gabriel sat together in the darkened interior of his sports car. He had parked outside the old Victorian building where she lived, only the moonlight from above illuminating the quiet residential street.

Apart from the fact that it wasn't raining, it was an end to the evening so reminiscent of the one five years ago. A memory that had remained etched in Bryn's mind.

She had been mooning about Gabriel for weeks by that time, totally infatuated with his dark good looks and confident air. After he had come to her parents' house to talk with her father a couple times, she had taken to calling in to the Archangel Gallery several times a week on the off chance she might see him again.

That evening she had hung around outside at closing time, telling herself it was because she was waiting for the rain to ease off before making a dash for the bus stop, but in reality she had been hoping to catch a glimpse of Gabriel as he left the gallery.

Her breath had caught in her throat when she'd seen him coming out of the main doors, a fiery blush on her cheeks as he'd looked up and seen her, his face going blank for several seconds before recognition had widened those chocolate-brown eyes and he'd stopped to chat with her. It had been a blushingly stilted conversation on Bryn's part, and she had been rendered completely speechless when Gabriel had asked if he could drive her home.

She had been so aware of Gabriel's proximity once they were seated in the confines of his sleek sports car, the silence between them on the drive to her home seeming heavy with possibility and causing Bryn to tremble with nervous anticipation.

She had given him a shy glance from beneath dark lashes once he'd stopped the car outside her parents' house. 'Thank you for driving me home.' She had groaned inwardly at her lack of sophistication.

'You're welcome.' His voice had been husky as he'd turned in his seat to look at her. 'Sabryna, I— Tomorrow there's going to be—' He had broken off, frowning darkly. 'Oh, to hell with it, if I'm going to burn I may as well go down in a ball of flames!' he had muttered fiercely before his head had swooped down and his lips had captured hers.

It had been the most exquisite kiss of Bryn's young life, slow and searching, but at the same time so erotically charged she had felt as if she might drown in the feelings, emotions, coursing through her body.

She had been totally dazed by those emotions as Gabriel had suddenly wrenched his mouth from hers to look down at her briefly with hot, passionate eyes before moving back and turning away.

'You should go in,' he muttered darkly. 'And try not to— Never mind,' he had bitten out abruptly as he'd turned to look at her with tortured eyes. 'I'm sorry, Sabryna.'

She had blinked. 'For kissing me?'

'No,' he had rasped harshly. 'I'll never be sorry I did that. Just— Try not to hate me too much, okay?'

At the time Bryn had believed she could never hate Gabriel, that she loved him too much to ever hate him.

The following day, that 'tomorrow' Gabriel had referred to so obliquely, her world had blown up in her face, as her father had been arrested for forgery, with Gabriel lined up as the prosecution's lead witness against him.

'I'm glad,' Gabriel murmured now in answer to her earlier comment.

Bryn came back to the present with a bump. 'I'd ask you in for coffee, but...' She trailed off with hard dismissal.

It had been a surprisingly enjoyable evening, Bryn acknowledged self-disgustedly, knowing that the past shouldn't have allowed her to enjoy an evening with the hateful Gabriel D'Angelo.

But she had....

The food had been so excellent and the decor, the crowded room and loud conversation had all become part of that enjoyment. Two glasses of wine and she had even become fond of Toni's off-key renditions of classical Italian arias!

As for the company... Gabriel had proved to be an amusing and entertaining dining companion, as they discussed their favourite artists as they ate, along with some of the funnier stories from Gabriel's years of running the Archangel Galleries with his brothers.

Bryn had felt totally relaxed in his company by the time they left the bistro, from the good food, the wine and the good company, so much so that it had seemed like the most natural thing in the world to agree to Gabriel driving her home.

Enjoyable as the evening had been though, she admittedly inwardly that she found Gabriel even more disturbing now than she had five years ago.

As Gabriel D'Angelo he was unmistakably intelligent, sinfully handsome, as well as being equally sinfully rich and powerful.

As Gabriel he was obviously intelligent and handsome, but he was also relaxed and charming, plus he had a slightly wicked sense of humour, and a warmth that had allowed him to accept, without so much as a blink, the enthusiastic kiss Maria had planted on his lips, with the plea to 'come back and see me soon', before they left the bistro earlier.

All of those things, together with those dark and mesmerising good looks, that Bryn had become so increasingly aware of as the evening progressed made her very aware that she was in danger of falling under this man's spell for the second time in her life.

'But?' Gabriel turned in his seat to prompt Bryn out of her continued silence.

She raised startled eyes. 'Sorry?'

'"I'd ask you in for coffee, but…"' he reminded her.

She smiled ruefully. 'That's a woman's polite way of saying thank you for the evening but now it's over.'

'You don't have any coffee?'

'I always have coffee.'

'Then why not invite me in?'

She blinked long lashes. 'I—well—it's late.'

'It's only eleven o'clock.' Although it was obvious to Gabriel that Bryn didn't want to invite him into her home, and he knew she was right to feel that caution, he wanted so badly for her to change her mind.

He hadn't thought it was possible, but his attraction to her had deepened in the past few hours and he was now desperate to taste and feel those plump lips that had been tormenting him all evening.

So desperate he moved to close the distance that separated them. 'Bryn—'

'Please don't!' She immediately held her hands up defensively, her eyes wide with alarm as she leaned back against the door behind her.

'Why not?' Gabriel prompted.

She ran the moistness of her tongue over her lips before answering him. 'Why ruin a perfectly good evening?'

He frowned darkly. 'My kissing you would ruin the evening?'

'Please, Gabriel—'

'But that's what I want to do, Bryn— To please you!' He closed the last of the distance between them as he pulled her gently forward into his arms before looking down at her hungrily.

'I can't!' Her eyes glittered with unshed tears, her hands still held up defensively between them, not pushing Gabriel away, but desperately trying not to touch him either. 'I can't, Gabriel,' she repeated achingly.

It was the despair in her voice, along with those unshed tears glistening in her beautiful eyes, that caused an icy chill down the length of Gabriel's spine as he stilled. 'Talk to me, Bryn,' he encouraged gruffly. 'For God's sake, talk to me!'

'I can't.' She gave another desperate shake of her head.

'I have to kiss you, damn it,' he said, wanting Bryn, but more than that wanting her to trust him.

With her body. With her emotions. With her past....

She looked up at him searchingly in the moonlight for several tense, timeless seconds, before she gave another slow and determined shake of her head. 'I really can't,' she repeated flatly.

'Not good enough, Bryn!' he rasped. 'Tell me you

don't want me to kiss you, that you don't want that as much as I do, that you haven't ached for it all evening, and I won't ask you again,' he encouraged gruffly.

Her throat moved as she swallowed convulsively. 'I can't do that either,' she acknowledged achingly, her voice carrying a desperate sob.

'You want me to make that decision for both of us, is that it?' he bit out harshly.

Bryn was no longer sure what she wanted!

Well… She was, but what she wanted—to kiss and to be kissed by Gabriel—was what she shouldn't want.

He was a D'Angelo, for goodness' sake. And no matter how charming and entertaining he had been this evening, underneath all that charm he was still the cold and ruthless Gabriel D'Angelo from all those years ago. To allow— To *want* to kiss and be kissed by that man went against every instinct of loyalty she had, as well as every shred of self-preservation she possessed.

Except… She couldn't escape the fact that the man she had met earlier today, the man she had just spent the evening with—the same man who made her pulse race and caused her body to be so achingly aware of everything about him—wasn't in the least cold or ruthless, but was instead hot and seductive. *That* man she desperately wanted and longed to kiss.

Which was utter madness, when she knew exactly how Gabriel would react if he knew who she really was.

'Please let me, Bryn.'

She couldn't breathe as she looked up at Gabriel, unable to make a move to stop him as his hands moved up to cup her cheeks and lift her face to his, feeling herself drowning, becoming totally lost in the dark and enticingly warm depths of his piercing brown eyes as his mouth slowly descended towards hers.

CHAPTER FIVE

BRYN MELTED AS Gabriel first sipped, tasted and then devoured her as he crushed her lips beneath his, hearing the low groan in his throat as her fingers became entwined in the dark hair at his nape. Her breasts were heavy and aroused as they pressed against the hardness of his chest, Gabriel having pulled her in as tightly against him as was possible in the confines of the car as he continued to kiss her with an ever-deepening hunger.

A hunger that Bryn couldn't help but feel in return, groaning low in her throat as she felt the brush of Gabriel's tongue against her bottom lip, light, questing, possessing as her lips parted and his tongue surged inside, licking and tasting, learning every nuance, every dip and curve, his hands a restless caress along the length of her spine.

Bryn broke their kiss, her slender neck arching as she felt Gabriel's hand push her blouse up, his fingers lightly caressing the bareness of her spine, her abdomen, before his hand cupped beneath the bared fullness of her breast.

The soft pad of his thumb was a light, sweeping torture across her aroused nipple, his lips a hot caress against Bryn's throat as pleasure coursed hotly through her body, heating, dampening between her thighs, as he captured her aching nipple between thumb and finger, squeezing lightly.

His ragged breath burned against her throat as his other hand moved to unfasten the buttons of her blouse, allowing his questing lips to move lower, his tongue a sweeping, hungry caress against the tops of her breasts before dipping lower as he sucked her aching, straining nipple into the moist heat of his mouth.

Bryn's head fell back against the headrest behind her, her fingers becoming entwined in the dark thickness of Gabriel's hair as she held him against her, the intense pleasure of the dual assault of Gabriel's lips and fingers against her breasts almost too much to bear.

Almost.

The pleasure was just too good, too exquisite, as it built higher, and then higher still, as Gabriel continued to draw deeply on her nipple, his tongue a moist and rasping caress against that burgeoning heat, rising higher, deeper, until she felt as if she would explode into a million pieces that could surely never be completely put back together again.

Never.

'Gabriel, you have to stop!'

Gabriel was so aroused by the taste of Bryn and the desire that had raged so deeply, so out of control between them, that it took him several moments to realise that her hands were now pushing against his chest, her face turned away from him as she struggled to free herself from his arms.

He backed off the instant he realised what she was doing; he had never forced himself on a woman in his life before and he certainly wasn't about to start now. He desired Bryn too much to ever want to do anything that she didn't want, ache for, as much as he did.

Gabriel's breathing sounded harsh in the confines of the car. 'Hell, I totally forgot where we were.' He gave a wince as he realised they were still sitting in his car parked outside the building where Bryn lived, and that although the side windows of the car were darkened glass, the windscreen certainly wasn't. 'I'm sorry, Bryn.' He ran an agitated hand restlessly through the dark thickness of his hair.

She avoided so much as looking at him as she straightened and refastened her blouse with hands that shook slightly, her face pale in the moonlight.

'Bryn?'

'Not now, Gabriel. In fact, not ever!' she insisted shakily. 'I have to go.' She turned to look out of the side window. 'I— Thank you for dinner. I enjoyed Antonio's.'

'Just not what followed?' Gabriel murmured knowingly.

Bryn gave a pained grimace. 'I'm sure you'll agree it wasn't the most sensible thing either of us has ever done—'

'Bryn, will you, for the love of God, look at me?' he rasped his frustration with the situation. 'Talk to me, damn it!'

She turned slowly, eyes huge and shadowed, her cheeks as pale as ivory in the moonlight. 'I don't know what you want me to say.'

'Don't you?'

She looked away from the intensity of his gaze. 'How about, this should never have happened?' She gave a shake of her head. 'We both know that already.'

'Do we?'

'Yes.' Bryn looked at him searchingly. 'Unless— Is this standard procedure? Did you think, expect, that I would be so grateful to be included in the exhibition at

Archangel I would——?' She broke off abruptly as she obviously saw, and recognised, the tightening of Gabriel's jaw and the anger now glittering in the darkness of his eyes.

'I'm getting a little tired of that accusation, Bryn.' He spoke softly, dangerously so. 'And no, kissing me isn't the price you're expected to pay for inclusion in the exhibition!'

She winced. 'I didn't exactly say that——'

'You didn't *exactly* have to!' Gabriel bit out harshly, wondering if he had ever been this angry in his life before. 'What the hell sort of man do you think I am? Don't answer that,' he immediately amended. He already knew what sort of man Bryn thought he was.

Gabriel had thought, believed, that after a rocky start they had managed to spend a relaxed evening together, that Bryn was starting to see beyond what happened in the past——starting to see him beyond that——and instead she now thought him capable of using his position as one of the owners of the gallery to—— What an idiot, what a fool he was, to think that Bryn could ever see him as anything more than the man who had helped to put her father in prison....

'You're right, Bryn. You should go inside now,' he growled coldly. 'Before you think of something else to say to insult me.'

Bryn hesitated, continuing to look at Gabriel searchingly, unable to read anything from his suddenly closed expression. 'It wasn't my intention to insult you——'

'Then heaven help me if you ever do mean it,' he muttered disgustedly.

She moistened her lips with the tip of her tongue. 'I was—— I just—— Our going out to dinner earlier, what happened just now, it was a mistake.'

'Mine or yours?'

'For both of us,' she insisted firmly. 'And I think it would be better, for the sake of the exhibition, if it didn't happen again. If we keep things on a purely business footing between the two of us from now on,' she added.

'As opposed to?'

'Anything less than a business footing,' she maintained determinedly.

Gabriel gave a grim smile. 'Do you really think that's possible after what just happened?'

Bryn wasn't sure a business footing had ever been a possibility between herself and Gabriel—and she was utterly convinced of it after her response to him just now. Gabriel had only needed to kiss her, to touch her, to caress her and she had forgotten everything but him and the moment. Nothing else had mattered at that moment. Nothing.

And it had to. It must. Because she wasn't about to allow herself to suffer the heartache of falling in love with Gabriel D'Angelo.

Not again.

Gabriel took in the stubborn lifting of Bryn's chin, the determined glitter in her eyes, and knew that she meant it when she said she wanted the two of them to go back to having a business relationship only.

If not for the reason she stated.

He was thirty-three years old, had been sexually active for almost seventeen of those years, and he was experienced enough to know when a woman desired him. And, whether she liked it or not, Bryn had been looking at him all evening as if she desired him as much as he desired her, and what had happened just now had been a direct result of that mutual desire. Bryn might wish it weren't so, might believe it was insanity on her part to be attracted to Gabriel while still carrying the pain of the past, but none of that changed the fact that she *did* want him.

Whether or not she actually *liked* him was something else entirely.

And that mattered to Gabriel.

Because he not only desired Bryn, he liked her. He had liked her five years ago too, even before he had seen her unshakeable loyalty to her father, and the quiet strength she had offered her mother as the two of them had sat together in the courtroom day after day.

Just as he admired Bryn's determination since meeting her again, her tenacity to succeed so intense that she had even been willing to become involved with the Archangel Gallery, to meet with at least one of the detested D'Angelo brothers, in order to achieve the success she so desired.

Kissing and embracing Bryn while knowing she didn't return that liking was not an option for Gabriel. Not with this particular woman. 'Okay, Bryn—' he nodded tersely '—if that's how you want it, then that's how it will be from now on,' he bit out abruptly.

She blinked. 'You're saying you agree to—to just a business relationship between the two of us?'

His jaw tightened. 'I believe I just said so, yes. Do you not believe me?' he rasped as she continued to look at him warily.

Of course Bryn believed Gabriel; why shouldn't she, when he had never done anything, five years ago or now, to give her cause not to believe he always did and meant what he said?

It was just— She didn't— Damn it! Part of her was actually irritated and hurt that Gabriel had agreed so easily to the two of them resuming a business relationship. Even if it had been her suggestion.

Which was utterly ridiculous. The exhibition wasn't until next month, and she knew from the things Gabriel had told her earlier—she had heard at least some of what he had to say—that she would be expected to go to Archangel often during the next few weeks, sit for photographs and provide the contents for the blurb for the catalogue, and to oversee and approve the framing of her paintings. And it would be far better, for everyone involved, if she and Gabriel could manage to maintain at least a semblance of politeness between the two of them during that time.

Bryn knew all that.

Logically, she accepted all of that.

Illogically, she knew that the attraction she had felt towards Gabriel five years ago might have been buried, might have remained dormant for those same five years, but that it was still very much alive inside her, and had only needed for her to see him again, to be with him again, for it to be rekindled.

To rage out of control.

As she had been out of control a few minutes ago, so much so that she had been balanced on the edge of orgasm just from the touch of Gabriel's lips and hands on her body.

What made it all so much worse, so much harder to fight that desire the second time around, was knowing that Gabriel obviously returned the attraction.

An attraction he felt for Bryn Jones. A desire he felt for Bryn Jones.

Because he wouldn't have allowed Sabryna Harper within ten feet of him!

Which was why the two of them couldn't do this

again, why they had to set down the rules right now for any future meetings between them. 'That's good.' She nodded as she bent to collect her shoulder bag from the floor of the car before turning to open the door.

'Wait there,' Gabriel instructed tersely as he turned, climbed out of the car and came round to open her door for her. 'My mother taught me it's polite, and safer, to always walk a lady to her door,' he explained as Bryn looked up at him questioningly.

A courtesy that Bryn wasn't sure, with her own lack of politeness to Gabriel just now, that she deserved. 'Once again, thank you for dinner and introducing me to Antonio's. It's definitely the place for pizza,' she murmured as she searched for her keys in her bag once they were standing outside her door.

He nodded tersely. 'I'm going away on business for a few days, so I probably won't see you on Monday.' He shrugged. 'But you've already met and like Eric?'

'Yes.' Was that sudden, heavy feeling in her chest disappointment because she now knew there wasn't even a possibility of her seeing Gabriel again on Monday? If so, then she was in more emotional trouble than she had thought she was. 'Are you going anywhere interesting?' she prompted conversationally.

'Rome,' he replied.

Bryn's eyes widened as she remembered Gabriel telling her earlier that he only went to Rome for 'pleasure'.

And, having stated that she was only interested in a business relationship with him, she had absolutely no right to show the least curiosity—let alone feel that curl of jealousy in the pit of her stomach—about the reason for his going there now.

And yet she knew she did.

'Bryn?'

She forced herself to look up and smile unconcernedly as she unlocked the front door of the house before stepping inside and turning back to face him. 'Enjoy Rome.'

'I usually do,' Gabriel accepted distractedly as he looked down at her searchingly for several long seconds, before accepting there was nothing else for them to say. He turned and returned to his car, part of him wondering if he had imagined the way Bryn had gone suddenly quiet after he had mentioned going away on business, and the slight edge to her tone when she did speak. And if he hadn't imagined it, what did it mean?

Not what he hoped it did, he answered himself derisively. No, all it indicated was that Bryn was relieved, because even the possibility of the two of them meeting again on Monday had now been removed. If he thought it had been for any other reason then he was only fooling himself; Bryn had made it more than clear what she thought of him a few minutes ago. What she believed had been his reason for kissing her.

When his real reason had been because he just hadn't been able to resist any longer. Hadn't been able to fight the fact that she was the last woman on earth he should get involved with because the need, the hunger he felt to taste her was too great. And she had tasted so damned good. She might try to deny it to herself, but she had responded to those kisses and made no protest when Gabriel had touched her breasts.

He now needed this time away from her, to put some distance—literally—between himself and Bryn. And hopefully, by the time he saw her again, he would have his desire for her back under his control.

It was several hours later—several hours and half a bottle of single-malt whisky later—as he relived the evening over and over in his mind, that Gabriel remembered he had told Bryn that he only ever went to Rome for 'pleasure'.

He wondered—hoped—that might be the reason for that edge to her tone.

'That looks amazing, Eric.' Bryn's face glowed as she looked admiringly at the silver gilt frame that had been put on the painting she always referred to in her mind as *Death of a Rose*. It represented so much more than the death of a single bloom, of course; it was symbolic of any death: love, hope, dreams. And, as they had hoped, the silver gilt frame was perfect against the misty background, the blood-red bloom weeping dew and petals onto the base of the canvas.

Bryn had spent most of her free time at Archangel the past four days, safe in the knowledge that Gabriel was still away in Rome. The highlight of each day had been the hours she spent in the cavernous basement of the gallery with Eric choosing the frames they thought suited to bring out the best in the ten paintings she was to exhibit at the gallery next month. This evening was no exception.

As far as Bryn was aware, Gabriel had spent those same four days—and nights—in Rome, no doubt indulging his every 'pleasure'.

Bryn had kept busy while at the same time determinedly not thinking of Gabriel, the evening they had spent together, or the ways in which he might now be indulging his pleasure in Rome!

And she wasn't going to think about him now either. 'It's perfect!' Bryn enthused as she continued to gaze at the painting in the silver gilt frame.

Eric nodded. 'Gabriel will have the final yay or nay,

of course, but I think he'll like what we've done so far. No doubt he'll change it if not,' he added ruefully.

Bryn's smile faded at mention of Gabriel. 'He will?'

'He has a really good eye for this stuff.' Eric shrugged.

'Better than you?'

'Much better,' Eric confirmed without rancour. 'All of the D'Angelo brothers do. They're the reason I wanted to work for the Archangel Galleries.'

Eric took the painting down off the wall where they had hung it so as best to appreciate the effect of the framing. 'Feel like going for a drink somewhere when we've finished here?' he suggested lightly as he stored the painting away safely.

'I—'

'I believe you'll find that Bryn doesn't believe in mixing business with pleasure.'

Bryn's heart stopped beating at the harsh sound of Gabriel's voice behind her. She whipped round quickly to find him standing in the doorway just feet away. And looking—

Looking more lethally attractive than when she had last seen him—if that was possible—his dark brown bespoke suit obviously designer label, his cream shirt and tie of the finest silk, his ebony hair slightly tousled in that just-got-out-of-bed style, his face tanned a deeper gold, intensifying the colour of his warm, chocolate-brown eyes.

No, his eyes weren't warm this evening. They were icy. Like a deep arctic chill.

An arctic chill that swept contemptuously over Bryn as the coldness of that gaze moved over her slowly from head to toe and then back again. Gabriel's top lip curled back derisively as he took in her casual appearance in a black short-sleeved T-shirt and black low-rider denims and a face that was completely bare of make-up. At the very least Bryn felt she looked like the penniless student she had once been—still was?—compared to Gabriel's expensive and sartorial elegance.

Bryn looked more stunningly beautiful than ever, Gabriel acknowledged irritably, her eyes glowing a warm dove-grey, her cheeks flushed with becoming colour.

At least, her eyes *had* been glowing a warm dove-grey, and there *had* been colour in her cheeks too, as she obviously enjoyed Eric's company.

Until she turned to look at Gabriel, at which point her gaze had quickly become guarded and her cheeks had paled.

His mouth tightened as he glanced across at Eric. 'If you've finished with Bryn for this evening, I need to speak with her for a few minutes.' It was a statement rather than a question, Gabriel having no intention of taking no for an answer. From either Eric or Bryn.

'Actually,' Bryn began tentatively, 'I—'

'I think it's best if we go upstairs to my office for this conversation, Bryn.' Gabriel held the door open pointedly.

Her eyes widened, her creamy throat moving as she swallowed then wet the dryness of her lips with the tip of her tongue. 'I— Yes, of course.' Her hands were gripped tightly together in front of her, knuckles showing white. 'A rain check on that drink, Eric?'

Eric gave a relaxed smile, obviously completely oblivious to the underlying tension between Gabriel and Bryn. 'No problem,' he agreed easily.

Which was perhaps as well; Gabriel had always had a healthy respect and liking for their London in-house art expert, and he would hate to ruin their working relationship by having to exert his executive power. 'Bryn?' he prompted tersely.

She grabbed her denim jacket and shoulder bag from a chair before hurrying across the room to join him, pressing her spine back against the door frame so as not to come into contact with him as she slipped out into the hallway, her expression apprehensive as she waited for Gabriel to join her.

An entirely appropriate apprehension, as it happened.

'Whisky?'

Bryn stood awkwardly in the middle of Gabriel's elegant office watching as he removed his jacket and draped it over a chair before moving to the bar in long, easy strides. They had travelled up in the lift together in complete silence. Bryn's apprehensive. Gabriel's grimly foreboding.

It didn't help that Bryn was still uncomfortably aware of how young and gauche she must appear to him, in her casual clothes and wearing no make-up, only to then chastise herself for even caring what, if anything, he might think of her appearance. Gabriel D'Angelo was one of the owners of the gallery where her paintings were to be exhibited next month, nothing more. She couldn't allow him to be any more than that.

'It's a little early in the evening for me, thanks,' she refused lightly. 'Unless you think I might need it?' she added uncertainly as she saw the hard implacability of his expression.

A hard implacability that showed her just how relaxed Gabriel had been on the previous occasions the two of them had met and spent time together....

Gabriel made no comment as he poured an inch of whisky into two crystal glasses before crossing the room and holding one out to Bryn.

The past four days had been successful ones for him as far as business went, but far less so on a personal level, as Gabriel hadn't been able to shake off thoughts and memories of Bryn. Of that last evening with her, when the desire the two of them felt for each other had raged so out of control.

As Gabriel had no doubt it would rage out of control again, despite the business-only arrangement Bryn had suggested and Gabriel had reluctantly agreed to. Gabriel had wanted this woman five years ago, and he wanted her still. A fact that had been brought painfully home to him after he had spent an evening with the beautiful Lucia while in Rome, and then politely walked her to the door of her apartment before leaving again, rather than spending the night with her as he would normally have done. He hadn't felt a shred of desire to bed the raven-haired beauty because Bryn was the woman he wanted. In his arms. In his bed. In his possession! And that was never going to happen while the events of the past were allowed to continue to lurk in the shadows between them.

'You're going to need it,' he confirmed gruffly. 'We both are,' he added with hard self-derision, taking a much-needed sip from his own whisky glass as Bryn's perfume, that heady spice and desirable woman, invaded his senses.

Her hand moved up and her fingers curled around the proffered glass, a hand that shook as she made no effort to drink any of it. 'How was Rome?'

'Beautiful, as always.' Gabriel stepped away from her to stand with his back to one of the floor-to-ceiling picture windows, needing to put space between himself and Bryn—between himself and that insidious perfume invading his senses. 'It took some persuading but I finally managed to acquire the two magnificent frescoes for the gallery that I went to look at.'

'Oh?'

His mouth twisted mockingly as he saw, and recognised, the surprise in her expression. 'I did tell you I was going away on business.'

Yes, he had, but Bryn hadn't believed him, after his previous comment. Not that it really mattered whether or not she believed him, then or now; it was none of her business what Gabriel had been doing in Rome for the past few days.

At the same time as she knew part of her wanted to know, had anguished over it during those days and nights, as to what woman, or women, Gabriel was spending his time with in Rome.

Nor did she feel in the least reassured about his mood now as she saw the grimness of his expression. 'So what was it you wanted to talk to me about?' she prompted with forced lightness.

'Sabryna Harper.'

CHAPTER SIX

'BRYN, SIT DOWN here, put your head between your knees and just breathe, damn it! Yes, that's right,' Gabriel rasped harshly, slamming his glass down on the coffee table before guiding Bryn over to an armchair to push her head down between her knees as she drew huge gasping breaths of air into her starved lungs. 'Damn it, woman, do you have something against my thirty-year-old single-malt whisky?'

Gabriel bent down to retrieve the glass from where Bryn had dropped it a minute or so ago as she'd looked in danger of passing out completely. He put the glass back on the bar and grabbed a cloth to soak up the golden puddle of whisky that had seeped into the pale carpet.

'What did you say?' He frowned as he heard her mutter something in the vicinity of her knees.

'I said,' she bit out succinctly as she raised her head to glare at him, her face deathly pale, eyes deep grey wells of anguish, 'I don't give a damn about your thirty-year-old single-malt whisky!'

'I doubt you'll feel that way when I take the price of the bottle out of the sale of your paintings,' Gabriel assured her dryly as he sat back on his heels.

'What sale?' she came back bitterly, sitting up in the chair now that the first danger of her fainting had obviously passed, her expression one of proud fragility. 'How could you do that?' she continued accusingly before he could answer. 'How could you just come out with a statement like that without—without giving me some sort of prior warning?'

Well, it hadn't taken long for her to recover from the initial shock, Gabriel appreciated ruefully. 'What sort of warning should I have given you, Bryn?' he challenged as he stood up to throw the sticky whisky-soaked cloth disgustedly down onto the bar. '"Oh, by the way, I think the two of us may have met before across a crowded courtroom"? Or, "You look a lot like Sabryna Harper, the daughter of—"? Do not collapse on me again, Bryn!' he warned harshly as her face took on a grey tinge, her chest barely moving beneath the black T-shirt as she breathed shallowly.

'I'm not about to collapse.' Instead, she stood up abruptly, taking a few seconds to steady herself before straightening determinedly, her chin held high. 'How long have you known?'

He quirked one dark brow. 'That Bryn Jones is Sabryna Harper?'

'Yes!' she hissed, jaw clenching.

Gabriel gave a dismissive shrug. 'Since the beginning.'

'Since...?' Bryn gasped, reaching down to grasp the arm of the chair as she felt herself sway again, despite her earlier claim that she wouldn't collapse again. She gave a shake of her head. 'You can't have done!'

Brown eyes looked across at her calmly. 'Why can't I?'

'Because— Well, because— Because you can't!' Her mouth firmed as she shied away from listing those reasons why. 'I would never have got this far in the competition if you had known who I was from the beginning!'

He shrugged, his shoulders wide and muscled in the cream silk shirt. 'Admittedly my brother Rafe advised against your inclusion, but I decided—'

'Your brother Raphael knows who I am too?' She stared at him in disbelief.

'You know, Bryn, we're going to get a lot further with this conversation if we work on the understanding that I invariably tell the truth. No matter what the consequences,' he added harshly.

And one of those consequences had been Bryn's father going to prison. An indisputable fact that hung between the two of them, unsaid but there nonetheless.

'It was Michael who recognised you initially,' Gabriel continued calmly. 'He saw you when you came in for an interview with Eric at the gallery that first day, and then he spoke to Rafe about it, who then told me.'

'Quite the secret little coterie of spies, aren't you?' Bryn snapped defensively, still completely thrown and befuddled by Gabriel's admission of having known who she was from that first day.

Something she was still having trouble absorbing. Because if that really was the truth, as Gabriel claimed it was, then he had chosen her as a finalist for the New Artists Exhibition knowing exactly who and what she was.

Had ogled her breasts, that first day here in his office knowing exactly who she was. Had taken her out to dinner at Antonio's knowing exactly who she was. Had kissed her later that same evening in his car knowing exactly who she was.

Which made absolutely no sense to Bryn whatsoever.

'I don't think insulting me, or my brothers, is helpful to this conversation either,' Gabriel drawled.

Gabriel had decided while he was away in Rome and thinking of her constantly that the truth couldn't remain unspoken between them once he returned to London. And if Bryn wouldn't tell him the truth, then it was up to him to do it.

Bryn so obviously disliked, perhaps even hated, Gabriel for the part he had played in her father's trial. Her desire now, her physical response to him, much as she might hate it, and him, was just as undeniable. And Gabriel couldn't see any way forward for the two of them if the truth of who Bryn really was continued to remain unspoken between them.

Of course, there was always the possibility that there was still no way forward for the two of them once they had spoken of it, but Gabriel knew they couldn't go on any longer with this lie standing between them, that the longer he allowed that omission to continue, the less chance there was that he and Bryn could ever come to any sort of understanding of each other.

'I asked you to trust me several times, Bryn, to talk to me,' he reminded huskily.

Her eyes widened. 'And this was what you meant? That I should trust you enough to tell you I'm really Sabryna Harper, William Harper's daughter?'

'Yes,' Gabriel bit out tautly.

Bryn continued to stare at him disbelievingly. 'That's the most ridiculous thing you've ever said to me!'

He gave a derisive smile. 'Nevertheless, it's the truth.'

She gave a dazed shake of her head. 'In what universe did you think that was ever going to happen?' Gabriel seriously expected her to— He had really thought that she would one day trust him enough to tell him, to confide in him. 'It was never going to happen,' she stated flatly.

He drew in a sharp breath. 'That's…unfortunate.'

'I don't see why,' she challenged scathingly. 'Luckily for you, you already have your reserve candidate for the

New Artists Exhibition, so no problem there once you've had the pleasure of kicking me off—'

'I'm not kicking you off anything, Bryn, and I resent the fact that you think it would ever be a pleasure for me to do so,' he cut in harshly, running an agitated hand through the darkness of his hair as he scowled. 'And why the hell would I do that, when you're far and away the best artist in the exhibition?'

'Why would you?' she repeated challengingly. 'I'm William Harper's daughter!' she reminded him—as if saying it repeatedly would help her to accept that Gabriel really did know, had always known, exactly who she was.

'And, as I've already stated, I knew that when you were chosen as one of the six finalists.'

Yes, he had, which again made absolutely no sense to Bryn. Her father's name was so shrouded in scandal that her mother had decided to distance them from it all by changing their last name after he had died. A scandal that had been connected to this very gallery and the D'Angelo name; she couldn't believe that Gabriel would ever want to risk the resurrection of that scandal by exhibiting the paintings of William's daughter. And certainly not intentionally.

She looked across at him guardedly, once again aware of how he owned the elegantly furnished office rather than the opulence dominating the man; Gabriel was such a force in his own right that he seemed to own the very air around him, no matter what his surroundings. Something that had been all too apparent during her father's trial—even the judge hearing the case had treated him with a deference and respect he hadn't shown to anyone else in the courtroom. Something that had no doubt added weight to the evidence Gabriel gave against her father.

Not that any weight had needed to be added; there had been no doubting her father's guilt, not only for attempting to sell a fake Turner, but for having commissioned the forgery in the first place, having paid an artist in Poland a pittance to paint the forgery and then attempting to sell it for millions of pounds to Gabriel and the Archangel Gallery.

'Bryn, even without Michael's help, I would have known who you were the first time I looked at you again....'

She looked up at Gabriel sharply. 'I don't see how when my name and appearance are so different from five years ago.'

He gave a humourless smile. 'It's unlikely I'd ever forget the young woman who glared her hatred across a courtroom at me for days on end. Those eyes alone would have given you away.'

Bryn had never forgotten him either, but for quite a different reason.

Gabriel D'Angelo had, quite simply, been the most charismatic and darkly intriguing man she had ever set eyes on. But it was more than that; *he* was more than that. Gabriel had awakened something deep inside the eighteen-year-old overweight and slightly shy Sabryna that had filled her night fantasies for weeks before her father's arrest, and months after the trial had ended.

The same fantasies that had filled all of her nights since meeting Gabriel again a week ago. The same desire that had awakened in her again, a few minutes ago in the basement, the second she had heard his voice behind her. The same desire that had caused her breath to catch in her throat when she'd turned to look at him. The same desire that raged through her even now, just from seeing how his cream silk shirt fitted so well over the broadness of his shoulders and tapered waist, the tailored brown trousers of his suit draping elegantly from his hips. This man—Gabriel—awakened that hunger inside her just by being in the same room with her.

'How is your mother, Bryn?'

She looked at him warily. 'Why are you asking?' she came back defensively.

He shrugged. 'Because I'd like to know?'

'My mother is fine. She remarried two years ago. Happily.'

'That's good.' He nodded.

'Gabriel, if this is some sort of guilt trip on your part—'

'It's not,' Gabriel cut in harshly. 'Damn it, Bryn, I have nothing—absolutely nothing—to feel guilty about. Am I sorry for the way it happened, the way your mother's and your own life were affected? Yes, I am. But your father was the guilty one, Bryn, not me. Am I sorry that he died in prison only months later? Yes, of course I am,' he rasped. 'But I didn't put him there. He put himself there by his own actions!'

Yes, he had. And part of Bryn had never forgiven her father for that.

Which was something *she* had to live with. 'You kissed me the night before my father was arrested!' she reminded accusingly.

He closed his eyes briefly before opening them again. 'I know that. And I wanted to tell you— Despite being warned by the police, and my lawyers, not to discuss the case with anyone, I almost told you that night! It almost killed me not to do so.' He gave a shake of his head.

'I don't believe you,' she breathed heavily.

'No,' he accepted heavily. 'I tried to see you, Bryn. Against the advice of my lawyers I tried to see you again, after your father was arrested, during the trial, after the trial. I tried, Bryn! I wanted to explain, to— I never wanted to hurt you, Bryn,' he assured earnestly.

'But you did it anyway.'

'I told you, I had no choice, damn it.'

Perhaps he hadn't, but that didn't stop Bryn from resenting his silence. From resenting the fact that he had kissed her that night. From resenting the fact that he had broken her heart the following day....

'I didn't want to see or speak with you again.' She gave an abrupt shake of her head. 'You had nothing to say that I wanted to hear.'

'I guessed that,' he said bleakly.

She breathed in deeply. 'So where do we go from here?'

Gabriel looked at her from beneath hooded lids. 'Where do you want us to go?'

To his bed. On top of his marble desk. On the sofa. Up against a wall! Bryn didn't care about the 'where' as long as Gabriel finished what he had started in his car last Friday evening. The desire she had felt then was nothing compared to what it was now, after days of not seeing him, not being with him.

And she hated herself for it. Hated that in spite of everything, she still felt that way, still wanted him!

She moistened her lips with the tip of her tongue. 'I need to know— Have these past few days all been some sort of sick game? An act of revenge for what my father—'

'I could ask the same of you!' he grated harshly, anger flaring in those deep brown eyes, lips thinned, a nerve pulsing in his aggressively set jaw. His body was rigid with that same tension, his hands clenched at his sides before he reached out to pick up the whisky glass he had put down earlier, drinking down the contents in one swallow. 'In fact, my brothers insist on it!'

'Then ask, damn it,' Bryn bit out shakily. He looked at her guardedly.

'Why did you do it, Bryn? Why did you enter your paintings in a competition being run by the gallery, the man, who helped put your father in prison?'

Bryn drew her breath in sharply, all the colour draining from her cheeks as the starkness of Gabriel's words hammered into her like a blow she wasn't sure she was ever going to recover from.

The truth was completely out in the open now, spoken aloud between them with no going back, and no fooling herself, allowing herself to indulge her desire for this man, by assuring herself that it was okay to do so because Gabriel had no idea who she really was. Because he did know. He had always known.

She avoided meeting that accusing gaze. 'The truth?'

That nerve pulsed in his clenched jaw. 'In the circumstances, I'll accept nothing less.'

Bryn nodded. 'I was desperate. I'm an unknown artist who wants more than anything to succeed, and the best way to do that is to be exhibited in the most prestigious private gallery in London.'

'Thank you,' he accepted derisively.

Her anger flared again at his obvious sarcasm. 'I was stating a fact, not giving a compliment!'

Gabriel knew that. Knew Bryn. Not as well as he wanted to, but he did know her as being determined, gutsy and proud. All traits he could admire. It was the beautiful and desirable that destroyed him!

'Heaven forbid you should ever do that,' he drawled, eyeing the whisky bottle longingly as he placed his empty glass down on the bar before walking away. The enigma that was Bryn might be enough to turn any man to drink, at the same time as that same man—namely Gabriel!—would be well advised to keep his wits about him whenever he was in her company.

'Yes. Well.' She turned to walk over to the long picture windows, hands thrust into the back pockets of her jeans as she stood with her back towards him, her spiky hair in silhouette. 'Believe me, nothing less would have induced me to come anywhere near your gallery or you ever again!'

Gabriel gave a wince. 'Perhaps a little less honesty on your part might be preferable after all.'

'What do you want me to do now, Gabriel?' she continued tersely. 'Quietly withdraw from the exhibition?'

'I've already said that isn't an option,' Gabriel bit out.

She turned back slowly, stance defensive, breasts thrust forward, hands in her pockets. 'Then what are my options?'

That was a good question.

Having made the decision to put an end to this pretence, Gabriel had gone over the possible scenarios of this conversation over and over again in his mind on his flight back from Rome.

There seemed to be only two possible outcomes.

Outcome one—the one that was undoubtedly the best one for Bryn—was that they would continue with the business-only relationship they had agreed upon, and she would exhibit her paintings in the gallery next month. Outcome two—the one that Gabriel disliked the most—was that Bryn would walk away now: from the gallery, the exhibition and from him.

There was a third outcome—the one that Gabriel wanted but knew was never going to happen. In that Bryn continued with the exhibition, and the two of them agreed to put the past behind them and continue from where they had left off on Friday evening!

An outcome that Gabriel knew to be pure fantasy on his part, following on from Bryn's blunt comment.

His mouth tightened. 'What's going on between you and Eric?'

She blinked, lashes long and dark around those dove-grey eyes. 'Sorry?'

Gabriel's days in Rome, persuading an elderly count to sell two small frescoes to the Archangel Gallery, had been something of an ordeal as his thoughts had constantly wandered to the problem of what to do about Bryn rather than concentrating on the task in front of him. And his flight back to England had been consumed with thoughts of the conversation he needed to have with her.

He had only called in at the gallery for a few minutes to drop off some papers in his office before going to Bryn's apartment. He had been surprised to learn from the night security that Miss Jones and Mr Sanders were still in the building. Going down to the basement and seeing Bryn there with Eric, obviously totally at ease with him, laughing with him—being invited to go out for a drink with him—had not improved Gabriel's already taciturn mood.

'If you decide to go ahead with the exhibition at Archangel, and the business-relationship rule, then that rule will apply to all employees of the gallery, not just me,' he bit out harshly.

Bryn gave a slow shake of her head. 'I don't— Are you suggesting— Do you think that Eric and I are involved? Romantically?' she added incredulously.

It had occurred to him, yes.

Eric Sanders was only a year or two older than Gabriel, and pleasant enough to look at. He was also an extremely well qualified and respected art expert, and Archangel was lucky to have him.

Even so, Gabriel knew that he wouldn't hesitate to find some way to dismiss the other man if it should turn out that he and Bryn were now 'romantically involved'.

Bryn stared at Gabriel D'Angelo in disbelief. This was the same man she had almost allowed to make love to her in his car just days ago, a lapse on her part that still made her feel hot all over every time she thought of it—and she had thought of it a lot since Friday evening!

Did Gabriel really think— Did he believe that she would have become involved with another man in the time he had been away in Rome?

'If you bothered to find out a little more personal information about your employees,' she snapped angrily, 'then you would know that Eric is engaged to a very lovely girl called Wendy, and that the two of them are getting married in three months' time!'

Gabriel nodded tersely, lids hooded over those dark brown eyes. 'As it happens, I do know that.'

Her eyes widened. 'But you still think that I— That the two of us have been— You don't think much of me, do you?'

Gabriel thought *about* this woman far too much than was comfortable. Or wise. Or conducive to a calm or logical frame of mind. Which was why he had jumped to the conclusion he had in regard to the friendly ease that obviously existed between Eric and Bryn!

None of which he was about to admit out loud to Bryn when she was this prickly and defensive. 'I'm tired and irritable and I haven't eaten yet this evening.'

Her eyes widened indignantly. 'And that's the excuse you're giving for accusing me of being involved with a man who's happily engaged to another woman?'

Gabriel gritted his teeth. It was definitely the only explanation he was willing to admit to at this moment; admitting his jealousy of the other man wasn't an option. 'It is, yes.'

She gave an impatient shake of her head. 'We seem to be veering off the relevant subject.'

He quirked mocking brows. 'My being hungry isn't relevant to you?'

'You've just dropped the equivalent of a bombshell on top of my head, by revealing that you've been aware from the beginning who I am, so no,' she snapped, 'your being hungry isn't of the least importance to me. Or the fact that you're also tired and insultingly irritable!'

He should have followed his first instinct when they had entered the privacy of his office a short time ago, Gabriel realised ruefully—which had been to strip Bryn naked, pick her up in his arms and carry her over to his desk to lay her down on the top of it, before making fierce and satisfying love to her!

That was what he *should* have done.

What he still wanted to do....

He now wanted that so badly, his erection so hard and aching against the soft material of his trousers, that the past few days might just as well not have happened.

Bryn eyed Gabriel uncertainly, her mouth suddenly dry as he began slowly stalking towards her, a determined glitter in the intensity of his dark gaze. 'Gabriel, what are you doing?' She took a step back, only to feel the cold of the window down the length of her spine as she stood flush against it.

'What I should have done the moment I saw you again,' Gabriel growled as he stood in front of her, the heat of his body not quite touching hers as his hands moved up to rest on the glass of the window on either side of her head, effectively holding her captive within the circle of his arms. His breath was a warm caress across her cheeks, those deep brown eyes holding—possessing—hers as she found it impossible to break away from the intensity of his gaze.

Bryn's heart was pounding rapidly in her chest, and she couldn't breathe, certainly couldn't have moved, even if someone had shouted 'fire'. Because the only fire that mattered to her was right here between the two of them as it blazed fiercely, heatedly, out of control.

'That might have been a bit awkward, considering that Eric was in the room at the time,' she said, attempting to lighten the tension currently sizzling between them.

'Do I look as if I care who else was in the room?'

The reckless glitter in his eyes answered with a resounding no to the question. 'You do realise that this—whatever this is—is only going to complicate an already impossible situation?'

He nodded briefly. 'And I'm currently in the mood to complicate the hell out of it!'

Bryn swallowed before running her tongue over her lips.

'Did you know you have a habit of doing that?' Gabriel murmured achingly.

'I do?' Bryn's voice was just as hushed; the whole building was so empty and quiet at this time of night, with none of the sounds from outside penetrating the thick glass behind her either, giving the impression that they were the only two people in the world. The only two that mattered at this moment.

'Mmm.' He nodded, gaze transfixed on her slightly parted lips. 'And every time you do it I want to replace your tongue with mine.'

'You do?' Bryn still couldn't move, her heart beating

even louder, faster in her chest, as a wave of heat washed over her, plumping the lips between her thighs, causing a fire in her belly, swelling her breasts, her nipples becoming engorged against her T-shirt, before that heat licked up the slenderness of her throat and coloured her cheeks.

'Mmm.' Gabriel gave another nod as he raised the fierceness of his gaze to meet hers. 'And the way I see it, you have two choices right now.'

She swallowed. 'Which are?'

He smiled slightly. 'One, you can take me away from here and feed me. Two—and this is my personal favourite—we stay here instead and indulge a very different appetite.'

Against her better judgement, the second choice was Bryn's personal favourite too!

Right here and right now.

Later—much later—she knew she would feel totally differently about that choice, but the two of them were caught in a moment seemingly out of time, where there was no past and no future, only now, her body expectantly aroused, aching with hunger. For Gabriel. For the touch of his hands. The feel of his lips against her skin. Everywhere.

She forced herself to make some effort at resisting that hunger. 'There is the third choice of my just walking away.'

Gabriel shook his head. 'Not this time.'

'But—'

'No buts, Bryn.' He rested the heat of his forehead against hers, those brown eyes now mesmerisingly close to hers. 'It's your choice, Bryn,' he assured huskily. 'But I advise that you choose quickly!' he added urgently.

Bryn felt surrounded by him, held captive by him—his physical presence, his heat, the sensual pull of that muscled body so dangerously close to her own—so much so that she knew that the choice had already been made for her.

CHAPTER SEVEN

GABRIEL FELT AS if time had stopped as he waited for Bryn to answer—an answer that, knowing Bryn, could very well be her deciding to knee him in the groin, rather than choosing either of the two options he had so arrogantly given her!

His only excuse for that arrogance was the need he felt, the burning ache he had, to make love to her—which he doubted the fiery Bryn would see as a reasonable excuse at all.

His jaw was clenched, his forehead slightly damp against Bryn's, his arms rigid as he kept his hands flat on the window on either side of her head. He continued to hold himself back from coming into contact with her body, his arousal a throbbing ache, his shoulders tense as he waited for her to speak. For her to decide, to choose, to determine what happened next.

Bryn's tongue flicked nervously across her lips, only for her to quickly bring a halt to the nervous movement as she saw the way the darkness of Gabriel's gaze was now fixed so intently on those parted and moist lips.

She breathed raggedly, unevenly, her gaze continuing to hold Gabriel's as she spoke in a hushed voice. 'I'm getting a neck ache just looking up at— What are you doing?' She gasped as Gabriel skimmed his hands lightly down her arms, placing them on her waist before moving down onto his knees in front of her. Bryn was forced to reach out and grasp onto the support of his shoulders as she tottered at the suddenness of the movement, Gabriel's eyes now level with her breasts. 'Better?' he murmured throatily.

Better wasn't quite the word Bryn would have used— she would have described their current position as *very* dangerous.

Gabriel was so close now, his face just a breath away, allowing her to see the fire in the depths of those chocolate-brown eyes up close and very personal, the darkness of his hair falling rakishly, enticingly, over his forehead, those sculptured lips parted oh-so-temptingly.

The warmth of his hands on her waist seemed to burn through the cotton of her T-shirt. Big hands. So much so that they almost spanned the slenderness of her waist completely.

Bryn had felt surrounded by Gabriel before, but now she felt totally overwhelmed by his close proximity, the burning heat of his hands on her waist, that same heart burning in his eyes as he looked up at her. 'You do realise this isn't going to change anything, right?'

'I don't want to change anything. I'm more than happy with exactly where we are right now,' he assured huskily, his hands shifting, gaze dropping lower to watch as his fingers slowly pushed up her T-shirt to bare the smooth and silky skin of her abdomen. 'Very happy, in fact….' he murmured throatily, his breath warm against her skin as his lips trailed lightly, caressingly, across her bared flesh.

This wasn't what Bryn had meant, and Gabriel knew it. But she ceased to care at that moment as her every thought, every sensation, came down to the feel of Gabriel's lips and the rasp of his tongue moving caressingly against her skin.

She gasped low in her throat, her back arching, her fingers tightly gripping on to Gabriel's shoulders as his hands now moved up beneath her T-shirt and cupped breasts covered by nothing more than a black lace bra.

'You are so beautiful, Bryn,' he growled softly. 'I've thought of doing this for longer than I care to think about—' he pushed the T-shirt higher so that he could kiss the tops of her breasts '—and this.' He pulled the T-shirt up and over her head before discarding it onto the floor, his eyes dark and hungry. He looked at her appreciatively for several seconds before reaching up to tug the lace cup of her bra down and bare one of her breasts, the rosy nipple already hard and pouting. 'And, oh, God, this!' he groaned, his hands resting on her hips as his mouth closed over the tip of that bared breast and he sucked her roused nipple fully into the heat of his mouth.

Fire surged and swelled inside Bryn, making it difficult for her to breathe at all as she felt that pull on her nipple accompanied by the rasp of Gabriel's tongue, the place between her thighs dampening as her fingers became entwined in the darkness of his hair and she held him closer to her, needing more, wanting more.

Receiving more as Gabriel deftly unclipped and removed her bra completely before suckling and feeding on her other nipple as his hand caressed its twin.

'Could we at least move away from the window? We can be seen from outside the building.' Bryn gasped in half protest, too aroused, too greedy for more, to be able to call a halt to this. Gabriel's breath was hot against the dampness of her breast as he reluctantly released her nipple. 'The windows are reflective. No one can see in. Only we can see out.'

'Oh. Ah!' Bryn gasped breathlessly as Gabriel's hands moved to unfasten the button of her jeans before sliding the zip slowly downwards.

He sat back on his heels, eyes so dark they appeared as black as the lace panties now revealed, the air cool against Bryn's heated flesh as Gabriel slipped off her trainers before slowly pushing her jeans all the way down her legs and removing them completely.

Bryn had never felt so exposed, so desired, as Gabriel glanced up at her briefly, searing her with a single, heated glance, his gaze moving lazily downwards.

Gabriel's hands moved beneath the black lace as he breathed in the scent of her, a perfume that increased his own arousal, demanding that it be set free, to claim what it already knew to be his.

A single glance at Bryn's face had revealed the flush of arousal on her cheeks, the feverish glitter in her eyes. Her fingers tightened almost painfully in his hair as one of his hands cupped her mound, shifting the black lace aside and allowing his fingers to seek out the bare flesh beneath.

Her curls were damp with arousal as his fingers moved lower before moving up and around the roused nubbin. Bryn gasped low in her throat, parting her legs as he slowly stroked her.

Gabriel wanted to taste her, to feel Bryn fall apart as she climaxed. He wanted, needed— 'You do know I just want to rip these panties off you?'

'You're the one who has too many clothes on, Gabriel,' Bryn complained, desperate to touch his naked flesh in the same way he was touching hers. She wanted to run her hands over his bared shoulders, explore the hardness of his chest and stomach, to taste the heat of his skin beneath her lips. 'Please, Gabriel,' she groaned achingly.

'Undress me,' he invited throatily as he sat back on his heels and looked up at her expectantly.

He looked so damned good, wild and seductive as a pagan god, with the darkness of his hair in disarray from her caressing fingers, eyes dark and glittering, his cheeks flushed, lips slightly swollen.

The admiration in Gabriel's eyes as he looked at her dispelled any embarrassment she might have felt at standing almost naked in front of a man for the first time.

Nevertheless, her hands shook slightly as they moved to undo and remove Gabriel's tie, unfastening the buttons of his shirt before pushing it off his shoulders and down his arms to fall onto the carpeted floor with her own clothes.

Bryn's breath caught in her throat as she looked down at his muscled shoulders, a deep V of dark hair covering his chest and leading down over the flatness of his abdomen before disappearing into the waistband of his trousers. 'You're beautiful,' she murmured appreciatively as her hands trailed lightly over all that muscled flesh.

'I believe that should be my line,' Gabriel came back huskily.

She smiled shakily. 'Not from where I'm standing.'

'Then let's not stand any longer.' His grin was entirely roguish as he stood up to sweep Bryn easily into his arms, carrying her over and laying her down on the sofa before straightening to strip off the rest of his clothes.

Bryn watched unashamedly as he slipped off his shoes and socks before unfastening his trousers and allowing them to fall to his feet, carelessly discarding them as if they hadn't cost what Bryn earned in a month.

She had thought him beautiful before, but, wearing only black body-hugging boxers that clearly revealed the lengthy bulge beneath, he had to be the most sinfully gorgeous man Bryn had ever set eyes on: wide and muscled shoulders and chest, his waist tapered, thighs lean and powerful, legs long and lightly sprinkled with dark hair.

Gabriel felt the painful swell of his shaft in response to Bryn's appreciative gaze on him as he hooked his fingers into his boxers before slipping them down his thighs and legs, and then straightening.

She drew her breath in sharply as Gabriel stood naked in front of her, her wide eyes darkening to gunmetal grey as she gazed up at him with open hunger.

A hunger Gabriel was powerless to resist as he stepped closer, his breath catching in his throat as Bryn reached out to trail her fingers lightly down the silken length of his shaft, her face flushed with passion as she traced the engorged blood vessels along the length to the bulbous tip.

Gabriel's jaw clenched, hands fisting at his sides, as Bryn sat up and swung her legs to the floor, her breasts thrusting temptingly as she leaned forward to curl her fingers about his erection, her tongue moving distractedly over her lips as the soft pad of her thumb touched the moistness of that sensitive purple head. She looked up at him briefly before slowly lowering her head and lapping up those escaping juices with the soft rasp of her tongue.

'Sweet—' Gabriel muttered as he drew in a hissing breath, his whole body rigid with tension. 'Are you trying to kill me, Bryn?' he choked as she continued.

'You taste delicious,' she murmured appreciatively. 'Sweet and yet salty too.' The fingers of one hand remained curled about him as she parted her lips before taking him completely into her mouth.

'You *are* trying to kill me!' Gabriel's back arched, his hands becoming entangled in Bryn's hair as he began to thrust slowly, instinctively, into that hot, moist cavern as

Bryn's throaty chuckle of satisfaction vibrated along the length of his pulsing and sensitive shaft.

Bryn hadn't known—had never imagined—anything could taste and feel this good. She felt bold, totally empowered by Gabriel's uninhibited response as her head bobbed in rhythm with his increasingly powerful thrusts, his hips bucking as those thrusts became more urgent still.

'You have to stop, Bryn,' he gasped, his fingers biting into the bareness of her shoulders as he halted her movements. 'Or I'm going to lose this before we've even begun.'

Her lashes rose as she looked up at Gabriel to find him looking down at her, his expression pained; eyes jet-black, cheeks flushed, his mouth twisted into a grimace.

Even so, Bryn was reluctant to release him immediately, moving slowly down his length, lips squeezing just beneath the purple head before she released that pressure. He gave a strangulated groan.

'Now it's my turn to torture you,' he added as Bryn finally sat back to look up at him with wide innocent eyes. 'And I warn you,' he murmured determinedly as he moved down onto his knees between her parted thighs before easing her back against the sofa, 'I'm not going to stop.' His head swooped down as he claimed one pouting nipple into his mouth, suckling deep and hard, as his other hand cupped its twin, finger and thumb plucking, gently squeezing.

Pleasure raged through Bryn like wildfire at this full-on assault to her senses, and she realised that Gabriel had only been teasing her earlier, tantalising her. Her head fell back against the sofa, back arching, as his mouth drew hungrily on her nipple, his thumb and fingers matching that wild rhythm on its twin as heat poured between her thighs like molten lava. The tiny nubbin there pulsing as her hips began to move against him restlessly, pleading, begging for Gabriel's touch.

He growled low in his throat before his lips released her nipple and moved down over her abdomen, his hands moving to grip her hips, holding her unmoving as his lips and tongue sought and easily found the nubbin pouting and swollen amongst her curls.

Her breath caught in her throat, heat engulfing her at the first caress of Gabriel's tongue across that sensitive bundle of nerve endings. He flicked his tongue mercilessly, again and again, across that pulsing nubbin.

Bryn sobbed low in her throat as her hips arched up in rhythm with that torturously flicking tongue, gasping, keening, as Gabriel's hand moved down and he slipped a finger inside her hot and grasping channel, gently thrusting. A second finger joined the first, her pleasure rising to fever pitch as his tongue flattened against her nubbin, pressing to the same rhythm as those thrusting fingers, until Bryn felt the pleasure rising, soaring, completely engulfing her, again and again, until she felt as if she had shattered into a million pieces.

'Are you okay?' Gabriel prompted with concern as he lay down on the sofa beside her and gathered her shaking body close against his.

Bryn in the throes of orgasm had been the most beautiful thing he had ever seen and heard; little throaty sobs had caught at the back of her throat, her face flushed, throat arched, breasts jutting proudly forward, her hips rising to meet each thrust of his fingers as the muscles in her channel gripped tightly with each prolonged spasm of pleasure. A pleasure that Gabriel had drawn out to the fullest until Bryn was sobbing and the tears flowed down her cheeks.

'I'm fine,' she answered him shakily, limp in his arms as she lay draped across his chest. 'Better than fine,' she added. 'That was the most amazing thing— I had no idea— It was truly amazing,' she repeated breathlessly.

'I aim to please, ma'am.' Gabriel chuckled softly.

'Oh, you did! You do,' she amended huskily, hand lightly caressing his shoulder. 'That was truly unbelievable. I— Are we going to stop now?'

'Not a chance,' Gabriel assured indulgently. 'I'm just giving you time to recover. You seem a little overwhelmed.'

'A little?' Her laugh was shaky. 'I could become addicted to so much pleasure!'

'You're doing wonderful things for my ego, Bryn,' he murmured wryly.

'I invariably tell the truth too,' she assured quietly.

Gabriel frowned slightly, not wanting either of them to dwell on the reason he had said that to her earlier, not when they were together so intimately. They could deal with the past, and the future, later; right now he just wanted to be with Bryn, with no tension or animosity between them. 'Didn't any of your other lovers pleasure you so well?' he teased.

Her fingers twirled in the curls on his chest. 'What other lovers?'

Gabriel stilled as he looked down at her searchingly, a smile of satisfaction curving her lips as she tweaked one of his nipples and watched as it hardened in response.

She looked up at him. 'Do you like that too?'

'I love it.' He nodded distractedly. 'Bryn—'

'Do we have to talk right now, Gabriel?' She moved to lay between his parted thighs as she flicked her tongue across his hardened nipple, causing Gabriel to draw his breath in sharply as his shaft once again jerked and swelled in response to the caress. 'You do like that,' she murmured with satisfaction, the heat of her breath brushing across his dampened flesh.

'Yes,' he grated between gritted teeth. 'Bryn—'

'Not now, Gabriel.' She glanced up at him pleadingly, her hands looking very pale and slender against his olive skin. 'I don't want to talk—to think—I just want to taste you some more.' She moved sinuously down his body until she knelt between his parted thighs and her hands both curled about the length of his shaft.

Gabriel sat up slightly as he reached down to grasp her wrists and stop those mind-numbing caresses before it was too late. 'Not yet, Bryn. I— Have you had any other lovers at all?' he prompted cautiously.

She frowned as she looked up at him. 'This isn't the part where we confess to past relationships, is it? Because I really would rather skip hearing about all your previous conquests!'

So would Gabriel; there hadn't been so many women for him that he didn't remember their names and their faces, but there had certainly been enough. Not so much during the past five years, but Bryn wasn't ready to hear the reason for that. 'We aren't talking about me, Bryn—'

'Well, we're not going to talk about me either, if this is going to be a one-sided thing!' she assured impatiently. 'Let go of my hands, Gabriel—'

He ignored her request. 'Bryn, are you even on any contraception?' he prompted exasperatedly.

She shrugged. 'I've never had a use for it. Don't tell me a man like you doesn't have a condom or two in his pocket somewhere? Weren't you ever a Boy Scout?'

'Bryn, will you please answer me?' Gabriel sat up, taking her with him, looking down at her intently as he continued to hold both her hands captive in his. 'How many lovers have you had?'

She blinked. 'Why do you need to know?'

'Because this is important, damn it!' he groaned. 'I really need you to answer the question, Bryn.'

She frowned. 'Am I doing something wrong? You seemed happy enough a few minutes ago—'

'I was very happy, Bryn. I *am* happy.'

'You don't look it.'

'That's probably because you keep avoiding answering my question,' he said, sighing his exasperation.

Bryn sat back, completely unconcerned by her own nakedness; Gabriel had seen and touched and licked parts of her that no other person ever had, so it was a little late for her to feel in the least self-conscious now. 'Are you going to make a thing out of this, Gabriel?' she prompted impatiently.

'That would depend on what "this" is,' he answered cautiously.

'Okay, let's just get this out of the way so that we can move on.' She sighed. 'No, I haven't had any previous lovers. Which actually answers your second question, doesn't it, because if I haven't had any lovers then I've obviously never felt the need for contraception either.' She looked up at him uncertainly as he released her to stand up abruptly. A nerve pulsed in his clenched jaw as he stared down at her.

'No lovers?'

'Not until tonight, no.' She slowly shook her head.

'Sweet mother of…' He ran an agitated hand through his already tousled hair as he began to pace restlessly. 'You should have told me, Bryn.'

'Why should I?' she reasoned. 'I should tell you that fierce pacing doesn't have the same impact when you're stark naked.' She fell silent as he quickly pulled on his briefs, trousers and shirt, not bothering to refasten the latter. 'Gabriel?'

He breathed raggedly. 'Just give me a minute, please, Bryn.'

'I believe there were two of us here tonight, not just me,' she continued despite his warning. 'And I don't remember you bothering to ask me any of these questions *before* we both took our clothes off.'

No, he hadn't, had he? Which was more than careless on Gabriel's part. His only excuse—if it could be called one—was that Bryn affected him so deeply he couldn't think of anything else but her when he held her in his arms.

He looked at Bryn now, still unsettled at learning that he was her first lover— Well, her *almost* lover. 'Bryn, I would have— I wouldn't have pushed so hard if I had known of your...inexperience,' he said gently.

She frowned. 'What does that mean?'

He shook his head. 'Well, I wouldn't have made love to you in my office, for one thing.'

'Why not?'

He closed his eyes briefly. 'Your first time should be in a bed, Bryn, preferably a four-poster—'

'I never imagined you as a romantic, Gabriel.'

His jaw tightened. 'Don't mock me, Bryn. Not now.'

'I'm not the one who just spoiled the moment!' She rose lithely to her feet, her face pale as she turned her back on him and began pulling her own clothes back on, her panties and jeans no problem, the bra proving less cooperative, forcing Bryn to thrust it impatiently into her pocket before she pulled her T-shirt on and fluffed out her hair.

'I could have hurt you, Bryn.' He gave a pained frown as he realised what he had just said.

'It's five years too late for you to think of that,' Bryn came back bitterly as she looked up from pulling on her shoes. 'Besides, I don't think either of us was thinking too clearly a few minutes ago. I certainly didn't think I needed to give you a list, or otherwise, of my credentials as a lover before we proceeded.'

He sighed as she stood up to collect her bag in preparation of leaving. 'You can't just leave—'

'Watch me.'

'Why are you so angry, Bryn? Can't the two of us at least talk before you go? Please, Bryn,' he encouraged gruffly.

Her mouth thinned. 'I don't think we have anything to talk about. We had an…encounter, and now it's obviously over.'

It hadn't just been an encounter to Gabriel. No matter what Bryn might think, how many previous lovers he might have had, he had never experienced anything even remotely like the pleasure he had felt with Bryn tonight. She was so beautiful she took his breath away. Responsive beyond belief. And the caress of her hands, the touch of her lips on his body, his shaft, had been so unbelievably arousing he had almost lost control.

He gave a shake of his head. 'I have the feeling that this was your first encounter too?'

Her cheeks warmed with colour. 'I've been a little busy the past five years, okay? Building a new life in Wales for myself and my mother. Getting my degree. Working to pay off the student loans, and the rent, and painting madly in my spare time. Besides which—' she drew in a ragged breath '—I would have felt compelled to explain about the past to anyone I became seriously involved with, and I've never cared enough to want to do that. I'm sorry if that makes me a lousy lover, but I—'

'You're not a lousy lover, Bryn,' Gabriel cut in forcefully. 'Far from it,' he added huskily. 'I just— I'm surprised that you chose me, of all people, to be your first.'

'You of all people,' she echoed bitterly. 'I suppose it is a bit ironic,' she murmured self-derisively. 'But it has a certain rightness about it too, if you think about it. You already know about my past, who I am, who my father was, which means I don't have to confess anything to you.'

In just a few short minutes everything between them had changed once again, and she was back to being her usual defensive and antagonistic self.

Or maybe that responsive woman was the real Bryn?

Gabriel didn't know anymore, and for once in his life he wasn't sure what to do next. Wasn't sure if there was any way they could move forward with Bryn in the mood she was in right now. 'Could we have dinner together tomorrow evening?' he asked tentatively.

Bryn's chin rose stubbornly. 'Not if it's going to result in us having some sort of post-mortem regarding what happened tonight, no.'

'Damn it, Bryn—' He broke off exasperatedly. 'I'm desperately trying to put things right between us, but I could really do with a little cooperation from you.'

'It's a little late in the day for that, isn't it?' she scorned.

'I'm really trying here, Bryn,' he bit out between gritted teeth.

She eyed him suspiciously. 'Put things right between us how?'

He sighed. 'We've skipped over a couple sequences

of a relationship, and I'd like to maybe take those two steps back and start again.'

Bryn looked at him searchingly, not sure where he was going with this. 'We had a sexual encounter, Gabriel, not a relationship.' An encounter that had been life changing for her, although she had a feeling that it was Gabriel himself who had made tonight so special; he was not only an exceptional and experienced lover, but a caring and considerate one too. Even with her own lack of experience Bryn knew that not all men were like that, so maybe she should be thanking Gabriel for the consideration he had shown her, instead of arguing with him.

And maybe she would be—if she didn't feel so confused about how she had allowed tonight to happen in the first place.

Nor did she understand why Gabriel had been thrown so off balance by her lack of experience; didn't men prefer no-ties-no-expectations sex?

And, damn it, she couldn't allow herself to become any more deeply involved with Gabriel than she already was. As it was, she had no idea how she would even begin to explain to her mother about her dinner date with Gabriel, let alone what had happened tonight; accepting another dinner invitation from him would only add to the complication of this situation.

'I appreciate the invitation, Gabriel,' she told him dismissively. 'And I understand what you're trying to say, but I'm really not interested in taking this any further.' She gave him a bright and dismissive smile.

'You're not interested in taking this any further?' he repeated slowly.

'No. You've said you're willing to forget the past, so I suggest we do the same with what happened just now. Let's both just forget it ever happened,' she repeated evenly.

Gabriel had never met another woman even remotely like Bryn Jones. Nor did he ever remember wanting to strangle a woman as much as he did Bryn at this moment.

First, she had aroused him so much that the two of them had almost had unprotected sex on the sofa in his office, of all places, and now she was giving him the brush-off. Unbelievable!

And was that injured pride speaking, or something else?

This woman had him so tied up in knots that Gabriel had no chance of sorting out his emotions. Except to know he wanted to see Bryn again, to be with her.

'Dinner tomorrow evening,' he repeated firmly.

'No,' she refused flatly.

Gabriel's eyes narrowed. 'You already have a date tomorrow night?'

Bryn raised her brows in silent rebuke. 'My shifts at work have worked out that I have three days off together, so I'm travelling home tomorrow morning to see my mother and stepfather. It's also the reason I was working late with Eric this evening,' she added challengingly.

'I see,' Gabriel murmured slowly, not willing to get into that conversation again, or the jealousy he had felt seeing her with Eric.

'How are you getting there?'

'By train.'

'Let me drive you—'

'Don't be ridiculous, Gabriel,' Bryn cut him off sharply, impatiently. 'It's bad enough that the two of us have met again. I don't need to shock my mother by having you turn up on her doorstep with me tomorrow.'

His mouth thinned. 'Are you saying she doesn't even

know about your participation in the exhibition at Archangel next month?'

Bryn snorted. 'I wouldn't even know where to start telling her of my reinvolvement with the D'Angelo family!'

'Damn it, Bryn.' Gabriel glared. 'Your mother never hated me in the way that you do—'

'You can't possibly know that,' she cut in dismissively.

As it happened, Gabriel did know that. But it appeared, from what Bryn was saying now, that Mary Harper had never told her daughter of their meetings after William went to prison.

'Bryn, your father—'

'I don't want to talk about him!' Her eyes flashed in warning.

Neither did Gabriel, but at the same time he knew it was a subject they couldn't continue to avoid. 'Bryn, he was a man, not a saint. Just a man,' he repeated heavily. 'His past misdemeanours weren't allowed to come out in court because they would have prejudiced the verdict, but surely you know that your father was a professional conman.'

'How dare you?' she gasped furiously.

Gabriel frowned. 'Not only that, but he brought about his own downfall.'

'You already said that!'

'But I mean this literally.' He sighed. 'Bryn, the reason I came to your home, talked to your father a couple times, was to try to talk him out of going through with trying to sell the painting. Because I knew, deep inside me, here—' he held his hand to his heart '—that the painting was a forgery. I had no proof but that feeling, but that was enough for me to try to stop him from going through with it. The morning after I visited him the second time the headlines of the painting's existence were blazing across half a dozen newspapers.'

'You're saying my father was the one who went to the press?' Bryn gasped.

'Well, I certainly didn't. And if it wasn't me, then it had to be him. If you don't believe me—'

'Of course I don't believe you!' she said scornfully.

He sighed heavily. 'Then ask your mother about him, Bryn,' he encouraged. 'Ask her to tell you about all the years she suffered in silence through William's schemes and machinations. Ask her if he went to the press. You have to ask her, Bryn,' he repeated forcefully.

'I don't have to do anything.' She gave a determined shake of her head. 'I think—' she breathed deeply '—that I may actually hate you for the things you've said tonight.'

Gabriel had no choice but to watch as Bryn left, accepting that if hate was all Bryn had to give him, then he would take even that hate.

CHAPTER EIGHT

'OKAY, YOUNG LADY, time to spill the beans!' Bryn's mother smiled as she placed a jug of fresh lemonade and two glasses down on the picnic table, joining Bryn. They sat outside in the garden at the back of the cottage where she now lived with Rhys Evans, her second husband.

'Spill what beans…?' Bryn straightened in her garden chair as she slowly pushed her sketch pad aside, her expression cautious as she watched her mother pour lemonade into the glasses.

Mary, a slightly older version of Bryn, with shoulder-length brown hair and deep grey eyes, gave her a reproving glance as she dropped down into a seat on the other side of the wooden table. 'This is your mother you're talking to, Bryn. And you've been here for two days already and barely spoken a word since you arrived.'

'I've been busy sketching.' Bryn had found it soothing to lose herself in drawing the beautiful array of coloured flowers that scented her mother's cottage garden, rather than think of the things Gabriel had said about her father before she left London.

'I noticed,' Mary dismissed. 'Now tell me who he is!' she prompted interestedly as she sipped her lemonade.

'He?' Bryn squeaked a reply. She should have known by now how impossible it was to divert her mother's attention once she had made her mind up to something—which she now seemed to have done on the subject of Bryn's distraction these past two days.

'The man who's making my normally chatty daughter so introspective.'

Bryn recognised her mother's tone as being the 'and don't try telling me any nonsense'—in this case, that there was no man—'because I won't believe you' tone.

And Bryn knew she had been unusually quiet since coming home to visit her mother and Rhys, that the last evening with Gabriel had left her in a state of confusion. About the things Gabriel had said about her father as much as about Gabriel himself.

She gave her mother a searching glance now. 'Are you happy with Rhys?'

'Absolutely,' her mother answered instantly, a warm smile curving her lips.

Bryn nodded slowly. 'And were you happy with Daddy?'

Her mother's smile faded and a frown appeared between her eyes. 'Where's this coming from, Bryn?'

'I don't know.' She stood up restlessly. 'I just— I've watched you and Rhys together, the teasing, the easy affection, the total respect you have for each other, and—and I don't remember ever seeing you and Daddy together like that.'

'We were happy in the beginning. When you were little.'

Bryn gave a pained frown. 'But not later on?'

Her mother grimaced. 'It became…complicated. Everything was fine to start with, but then William became restless working in an office day after day, and started coming up with these get-rich-quick ideas—all of which failed miserably. You're old enough to know these things now, Bryn. William used up all our savings on those ideas, and I never knew what he was going to do next. Or whether we would all still have a roof over our heads the following week.' She shrugged. 'That sort of uncertainty in a partner can test even the best of relationships to its limits, and our marriage was already pretty shaky. It very quickly deteriorated into chaos.'

Which was probably why her mother now appreciated Rhys's steadiness, Bryn's stepfather having been the local and much-respected carpenter for all of his working life.

'But you stayed together....'

Her mother smiled. 'We had you.'

'But did you never think of leaving Daddy?' Bryn looked at her mother searchingly.

'Many times,' Mary admitted truthfully. 'And I'm sure, as much as it would have hurt you, it would have come to that in the end.'

Bryn gave a pained frown. 'And yet, even during the trial, you stood by him.'

'He was my husband. And your father,' her mother added pointedly. 'And you adored him.'

Yes, Bryn had adored her father. But she hadn't been able to get Gabriel's outburst that last evening in London out of her mind. To question, to want to know if the things he had said were true.

Her mother's comments confirmed what Bryn had feared—that William had been the petty crook Gabriel had called him, for almost all of her life, involved in one scam or another. A petty crook who had tried to break into the big time by selling the fake Turner—and failed miserably.

And these past few days Bryn had questioned whether she hadn't always known that, and that it was the knowing that had added to her resentment of Gabriel, not because he had kissed her, not because she had fallen in love with him, not even because of his involvement in her father's downfall, but because that involvement had made him part of the disenchantment she hadn't wanted to acknowledge all these years.

'Why the interest in all of that now, Bryn?' her mother prompted softly, her gaze sharp. 'Has something happened? Something that's made you start thinking, questioning the past?'

Gabriel D'Angelo was what had happened! A man who was making it impossible for Bryn not to question the past. But it wasn't Gabriel's fault; Bryn was the one who had chosen to come into contact with him again when she'd entered the exhibition.

No, it wasn't Gabriel's fault, but Bryn's reaction to meeting him again, her response to him, had set in motion those same feelings of guilt inside her that she had felt five years ago when she had looked across that crowded courtroom and known that, despite everything he was saying and all the damage he was causing to her father and her family, she still wanted him.

It had been bad enough then for Bryn to realise she was infatuated with the arrogant and handsome Gabriel D'Angelo, but she found it harder still to realise, all these years later, that she was still attracted to the man who had helped shatter her world.

Admittedly her mother was happily remarried, but still the past had to overshadow, to make impossible, there ever being any sort of relationship between Bryn and Gabriel. A relationship she would have to tell her mother about.

Even if her traitorous body seemed to have other ideas on the subject!

Just thinking about that last evening with Gabriel, of the depth of intimacy the two of them had shared, the way she had totally fallen apart in his arms, climaxing so spectacularly, was enough to make her blush.

'Okay, now I really want to know who this man is if he can make my sensible daughter blush so prettily,' her mother stated firmly.

'I can't tell you,' Bryn groaned.

'Why on earth not?' Mary looked stunned. 'We've always been able to talk about anything in the past— Bryn, if it's a woman making you feel this way, then I hope you know that I'm broad-minded enough not to—'

'It's not a woman!' She gave a rueful smile. 'But I appreciate knowing how broad minded you are!' she added dryly.

'Is this man involved with someone else, then? Maybe married?' her mother added worriedly.

'It's worse than that!' Bryn groaned as she began to pace the lawn Rhys had recently cut. Her mother's brows rose. 'What could possibly be worse than—? Is he older than you?'

'Marginally.' Bryn shrugged. 'Maybe ten years or so.'

'That's nothing.' Her mother sighed her relief. 'But I still don't understand why you won't tell me who he is.'

'Because I can't.' She sighed heavily. 'He's just not— suitable for me to be involved with, okay?'

'No, of course it's not okay, Bryn.' Mary frowned worriedly. 'I've never known you to— He isn't a drug dealer or something like that, is he?'

'Of course not,' Bryn denied ruefully.

Her mother didn't look reassured. 'But he's unsuitable in some other way?'

'Oh, yes,' Bryn sighed.

Mary continued to look at her searchingly for sev-

eral long minutes, that worried frown between her eyes.
'Does your interest just now, in the past, have anything
to do with your reluctance to talk about this man?' she
finally prompted.

'I— Maybe.' Bryn's teeth worried her bottom lip. 'Do
you know—? Is it possible that Daddy was the one to
tell the press about the painting, as a way of ensuring
the D'Angelo gallery, or some other gallery, couldn't just
dismiss the painting as a forgery?'

'More than possible, I'm afraid,' her mother sighed.
'You know, Bryn,' she said slowly, evenly, 'it took me
years to accept this, but your father was responsible for
everything that happened to him.' Exactly the words Gabriel had used to Bryn just days ago.

'Not me. Not you,' her mother continued firmly. 'Not
anyone else involved in that mess. Just your father. He
gambled not just with his own future but with ours too,
and he lost. We all lost. But having met Rhys, finding
such happiness with him, has shown me that we don't
have to continue to let ourselves be the losers, darling.'

'I'm not a loser—'

'Bryn, I've watched the way you've avoided all involvement with men these past five years,' her mother
admonished gently. 'And I'm telling you now that the
only way of allowing yourself to go forward is to let go
of the past.'

Tears blurred Bryn's vision. 'Sometimes that's easier
said than done.'

'But it can be done.' Her mother reached out and
grasped Bryn's hand tightly in hers. 'I'm living proof
of that.'

Yes, her mother's happiness with Rhys now *was* living proof of that. Except... Gabriel had been directly
involved in that past her mother spoke of. Not as a spec-

tator, or someone removed from the situation, but as a full participant.

'We'll see.' She squeezed her mother's hand reassuringly. 'But could we just forget about this for now? Talk about something else?'

Her mother looked less than happy with the idea. 'If that's what you really want.'

'It is.'

Mary nodded. 'You know where I am when and if you want to talk.'

Yes, Bryn knew; she just couldn't see a time she would ever be able to tell her mother of the emotional tangle she had got herself into with Gabriel.

'Did you have a good time in Wales last week?' Gabriel's expression was guarded as he looked down at Bryn and saw the way the colour drained from her cheeks. She slowly looked up from the magazine she was reading at the back of the coffee shop, the girl who had prepared his coffee having told him where Bryn was sitting taking her evening break.

Gabriel knew that Bryn had to have been back in London for four days now, but she hadn't come anywhere near the gallery, or him. Mainly him, Gabriel suspected.

The fact that his unexpected appearance at the coffee shop this evening had caused Bryn's face to pale so dramatically, as well as striking her uncharacteristically dumb, would seem to confirm that suspicion.

He pulled out the chair opposite hers and sat down before placing his mug of coffee down on the table between them. 'Everything all right at home?'

Her throat moved as she swallowed before answering him. 'Fine, thank you.'

'That's good.' Gabriel leaned back in the chair to

stretch his long legs out in front of him as he continued to study Bryn.

She appeared somehow fragile to his critical gaze. Her face was pale, and there were hollows in her cheeks that hadn't been there a week ago, implying that she had lost weight since he saw her last. Her eyes were also shadowed and bruised-looking, as if she hadn't been sleeping well.

Because she had been as disturbed by what had happened between the two of them the previous week as Gabriel still was, rather than the things he had said to her?

Had she talked to her mother, as he had advised? Did she now know the truth where her father was concerned? Or did she still hold Gabriel responsible for everything that had happened in the past?

His determination to find answers to these questions had brought him to the coffee shop.

The past week had been a torturous hell for Gabriel, the first three days spent wondering if Bryn would talk to her mother, what she was thinking if she had, what decision she was going to come to in regard to the two of them while she was away. He had then spent the four days since she'd returned from Wales assuming she had decided to cut him out of her life.

A totally unacceptable decision as far as Gabriel was concerned.

Bryn was totally disconcerted at Gabriel's arrival in the coffee shop, not least because his appearance, in a casual cream polo shirt, faded jeans resting low on lean hips and the darkness of his overlong hair falling casually over his forehead, had literally taken her breath away. How she wanted this man.

More so even than a week ago, she acknowledged achingly as she looked at him from beneath lowered lashes, their time together in Gabriel's office, the intimacies they had shared, having for ever changed the way she now thought and felt about him.

A realisation that made a complete nonsense of her avoidance of him this past week.

'You haven't been to the gallery since you got back.' Gabriel's accusing tone echoed some of her thoughts.

She shrugged. 'I've spoken to Eric several times on the phone, explained that I couldn't make it to the gallery because I've been really busy at work.'

'So he told me.'

Bryn found it impossible to meet the dark shrewdness of Gabriel's gaze. 'Then I don't understand why you're here.'

He lost his relaxed pose as he sat forward and grasped both of her hands in his, his nostrils flaring angrily as Bryn instinctively sat back and tried to pull free. A freedom he wouldn't allow her. 'I'm here so that we can have the conversation we didn't finish a week ago.'

Her tone was pleading. 'Gabriel—'

'Bryn, don't try to freeze me out, or put me, and what happened between us, into some convenient little compartment in your brain never to be opened again,' he warned fiercely, 'because, I assure you, that isn't going to happen. I'm not going to allow it to happen.'

She gave another tug on her hands, once again failing to free herself, her throat moving as she swallowed before speaking. 'I don't know what you mean—'

'Like hell you don't,' Gabriel scorned harshly.

A blush warmed her cheeks as she hissed, 'You're causing a scene, Gabriel.' Several people at neighbouring tables had turned to give them curious glances as they had obviously heard the harshness of Gabriel's tone.

He gave a humourless smile. 'We wouldn't be having

this conversation here at all if you hadn't been too much of a coward to come to Archangel when you got back.'

She gasped. 'I told you, I've been really busy at the coffee shop since I returned—'

'Too busy to so much as bother to telephone the man who is your lover?'

'Gabriel!' she warned fiercely, wrenching her hands painfully from his grasp even as she glanced around them before turning back to glare across the table at him. 'You are *not* my lover.'

'More than any other man has ever been,' he stated uncompromisingly.

And how Bryn regretted ever allowing Gabriel to realise that.

Gabriel wasn't enjoying this conversation, not his own part in it, or the fact that it was obviously causing Bryn discomfort. But this past week of not personally hearing so much as a word from her had made him so frustrated that he couldn't seem to help himself.

Just looking at Bryn again as she sat alone in a corner at the back of the coffee shop reading a magazine, taking in the delicate softness of her cheek, the long sweep of her lashes, the silkiness of that defensively spiky hair, had been enough to cause his breath to catch in his throat and his shaft to become hard and aching beneath his jeans—the same painful state of arousal he had been in for most of the past week!

Consequently, he wasn't in the mood to accept the brush-off from Bryn again. 'What time do you finish here tonight?' he prompted.

She blinked. 'Gabriel—'

'We either have this conversation at my apartment later tonight, Bryn, or right here and right now, but we are going to talk sometime this evening,' he assured her.

She gave a shake of her head. 'I'm tired, Gabriel.'

'And you think I'm not?'

Her frown was pained. 'I don't understand.'

'I haven't exactly been sleeping like a baby for the past week as I waited to see what you decided to do about us.'

'There is no "us",' she sighed wearily.

'Oh, yes, Bryn, there most definitely is an "us".'

She gave a shake of her head. 'Doesn't the fact that I haven't bothered to contact you since I returned speak for itself as to how I feel about what happened between us?'

Gabriel gave a humourless smile. 'It tells me you're a coward, nothing more.'

Her chin rose. 'That's the second time you've called me a coward in as many minutes, and I don't like it.'

'Then prove that you aren't one by meeting me once you've finished work tonight.'

She gave him a pitying glance. 'We aren't children playing a game of dare, Gabriel.'

'We aren't children at all, which is why you should stop behaving like one.' His eyes glittered angrily. 'I'm not going anywhere, Bryn, so if you thought I was going to help you get through this situation by going along with pretending last week didn't happen, you were obviously mistaken. It happened, Bryn. I suggest you live with it.'

Bryn had been living with it for the past week. With the knowledge of her complete lack of resistance to this man. With the fact that she'd had no control over what had happened between them in his office a week ago. With the fact that Gabriel had been the one to call a halt to their lovemaking because she hadn't been able to do so.

With the fact that she had only needed to look at Gabriel again tonight to know that she wanted him still.

Her mouth tightened. 'It would have been the gentlemanly thing to do, in the circumstances.'

'Insulting me isn't going to make me get up and walk out of here either, Bryn,' he assured her softly. 'This is way too important for that. To both of us. This past week, waiting, wondering, has been sheer bloody hell.' He ran an agitated hand through his hair.

She looked across at Gabriel searchingly, noting the dark shadows beneath his eyes, the sharp blade of his cheekbones above slightly hollow cheeks, lines etched beside his nose and mouth that she was sure hadn't been there before, and realised that this past week really hadn't been any easier for Gabriel than it had been for her.

'Why won't you just accept that I can't do this, Gabriel?' she groaned achingly.

'Because neither of us knows what this is yet,' he maintained stubbornly. 'And I'm not willing to just give up on it until we do know.'

She gave a shake of her head. 'Isn't it enough that we both know that the events of the past makes this impossible?'

'I refuse to accept that.' His gaze was tormented as he reached across the table to once again take one of her hands in his.

'You have to! We both do.'

Gabriel gave a shake of his head. 'Did you speak to your mother?'

'About you?'

'Obviously not about me,' he drawled knowingly at her shocked expression. 'But did you at least ask her to confirm the things I told you about your father?'

'And what if I did?' Colour warmed her cheeks as she avoided meeting his gaze. 'Knowing who and what my father was, the things he did, changes nothing, Gabriel.'

'It means we can put the past where it belongs—in the past! It can't be undone, or remade, because it is what it is, but if we— If we want each other enough, we should be able to talk about it, to get by it. And I do want you, Bryn, and the trembling of your hand when I touch you is enough to tell me that you still want me too.' His fingers tightened about her shaking ones as she would have pulled away. 'Nothing else matters at this moment but that.'

'And what about later? What happens once the—the wanting has all gone, Gabriel?' Tears glittered in her eyes. 'What happens then?'

'Who says it's ever going to be gone?'

'I do.'

'Then we deal with later when later comes along,' he stated firmly. 'For now I just want us to be together and see where this takes us. Can we do that, do you think?' The soft pad of his thumb caressed the back of her hand as he looked across at her intently.

Could they? This past week had been absolute hell for Bryn too, her desire for this man taking over her every thought as she remembered how it had been between them that night in Gabriel's office. The way they had still responded to each other despite both knowing who the other was, before her feelings of guilt had once again made her deny that desire she still felt for him. A desire that Gabriel so obviously reciprocated and refused to dismiss. Refused to allow her to dismiss.

Could the two of them really have a relationship for however long these feelings lasted and simply ignore the pain of the past?

Could she do that?

CHAPTER NINE

'COME IN AND make yourself at home, Bryn, and I'll pour us both a glass of wine,' Gabriel encouraged huskily as she stood hesitantly in the doorway to the sitting room of his apartment.

He had felt an inner sense of relief earlier, when Bryn had finally capitulated to the idea of the two of them meeting up again when she finished work at ten; he might have deliberately given her the impression he was both confident and unyielding in his demand for them to talk this evening, but inwardly he hadn't been at all sure, until that moment, that Bryn would agree.

Gabriel had been waiting outside in his car for her when she and several of her co-workers left the coffee shop a little after ten o'clock, the two of them not speaking after he climbed out of the car and opened the passenger door for her to get in, or during the short drive to his apartment.

She *had* lost weight, he realised as Bryn finally entered the sitting room, the black denims she wore not quite as figure-hugging as they had been a week ago, her collarbone visible at the open neck of her black shirt, those grey eyes appearing huge in the paleness of her face. Evidence that she was finding fighting the attraction between them as difficult as he was? Gabriel certainly hoped so, because this past week of not seeing her since the two of them had made love together had been sheer torture.

His expression softened as Bryn sank down wearily into the comfort of one of the brown leather armchairs. 'Busy evening?' he prompted as he poured two glasses of pinot grigio.

'Very.' Bryn accepted one of the glasses before taking a welcome sip. 'You have a nice apartment,' she added with an appreciative glance at the obviously masculine decor and original artwork on the walls.

'It isn't mine particularly.' He shrugged. 'We all use it whenever we're in London— Don't worry, Bryn, Michael and Raphael aren't in London at the moment,' he added ruefully as she instantly looked alarmed. 'Michael is in Paris, Raphael in New York.'

Her frown eased slightly. 'They really are wonderful names.'

He nodded. 'The family estate in Berkshire is called Archangel's Rest—and, I assure you, I've heard all the jokes.'

She smiled slightly but it quickly faded. 'Gabriel, I only came back with you tonight because I agree that we need to dispense with this situation once and for all, and then just move on— What are you doing?' she gasped as Gabriel put his glass down on the coffee table before kneeling down at her feet and beginning to unfasten the laces on her shoes.

He looked up to quirk a teasing brow. 'Removing your shoes, obviously.'

'Why?' She tried, and failed, to pull her foot from his grasp as he slipped one shoe off before turning his attention to the other.

Gabriel sat back on his heels after removing the second shoe. 'I'm guessing your feet ache from all that standing?'

'Yes.'

He nodded. 'Then a foot massage should be very welcome about now.'

'A foot— Gabriel, stop that.' She tried to pull away as he took one of her bare feet into both his hands and began to gently knead the aching flesh. 'Gabriel!' Her protest was less convincing this time, and she gave a low sigh of pleasure as his fingers continued to massage the tension from her tired muscles.

'Good?' he prompted.

'Oh, yes.' Her head fell back against the chair, lashes fanning over her cheeks as her lids closed and Gabriel continued to knead and massage her foot.

She had tiny elegant feet, the nails painted a bright— and defiant—red, Gabriel noted indulgently as he turned his attention to her other foot and continued to massage her aching muscles.

Bryn knew she should stop Gabriel doing what he was doing, that his kneeling at her feet was intimate enough, without the sensuous touch of his long fingers massaging her to add to that dangerous intimacy.

She *should* stop him.

But she couldn't.

Because she didn't want to; she was enjoying this far too much to want Gabriel to ever stop.

She had never thought of her feet as being an erogenous zone before now, but they obviously were, the warmth emanating from Gabriel's caressing hands now moving to other parts of her body, her nipples becoming hard and full, a familiar warmth between her thighs. 'You should think about taking this up professionally,' she murmured appreciatively, eyes still closed. 'You could make a fortune!'

Gabriel chuckled throatily. 'I already have a fortune. Besides which,' he added, fingers moving lightly over her ankles and calves now, 'I have no interest in massaging anyone else's feet but yours.'

Bryn raised one lid, her heart beating a loud tattoo in her chest as Gabriel looked back at her, those brown eyes once again as compelling and addictive as chocolate. An addiction Bryn was once again finding hard to resist.

'I think that's enough of that, thank you.' She pulled her feet out of Gabriel's grasp before bending her knees and drawing her legs up into the chair—well away from Gabriel's caressing hands. Her pulse raced as he made no effort to get up from kneeling in front of her. 'It's getting late, Gabriel,' she prompted determinedly. 'I need to leave soon.'

Gabriel sat back on his heels, looking up at her. 'Did you tell your mother that the two of us had met up again?'

'Did I—?' Her eyes had widened. 'Of course not!' Bryn protested impatiently.

His eyes narrowed. 'Why not?'

'Don't be obtuse, Gabriel,' she snapped, glad now that he wasn't still touching her. Because if he had been he would have been able to feel the way just being this close to him caused her to tremble in awareness. 'My mother never knew— She didn't know that we knew each other five years ago. I—I never told anyone about—about that evening you drove me home from the gallery.'

'The evening I kissed you.'

She grimaced. 'I'm surprised you even remember that.'

'It was too memorable to ever forget,' he assured gruffly.

Bryn looked at him sharply. 'I somehow doubt that very much.'

Gabriel looked straight back at her with hot, glittering eyes. 'The timing was all wrong, the circumstances impossible, but even then I wanted to do so much more than kiss you.'

'I— You did?' She was totally flustered by his admission.

He shrugged. 'I was attracted to you then. I'm attracted to you now.'

Bryn gave a scathing snort. 'Five years ago I was a chubby and gauche teenager wearing heavy-framed glasses.' And this man had been lean and sophisticated, with the same dark and wicked good looks that still took her breath away.

He nodded. 'And now you're sleek and elegant, and I'm guessing you wear contact lenses?'

She nodded distractedly. 'Except for when I paint, when I prefer to wear the glasses you returned to me last week.'

'You weren't chubby five years ago, Bryn, you were voluptuous,' he assured her earnestly. 'And your eyes were just as stunningly beautiful behind those glasses as they are tonight.'

She gave a dismissive shake of her head. 'We're veering off the subject, Gabriel.'

'Which is?'

'That just thinking about the distress it would cause my mother if I were to tell her I've met you again now, let alone this—this attraction, between us, is the very reason why it can't continue.'

Gabriel looked up. 'You can't possibly know how your mother would react.'

Bryn frowned her impatience. 'Get real, Gabriel, and

try to imagine how that conversation would go. "Oh, by the way, Mum, guess who I almost had sex with a couple nights ago. Gabriel D'Angelo. How weird is that?"'

Gabriel drew in a sharp breath before pushing up onto his feet to pick up his glass of wine, taking a sip before answering her, knowing Bryn was now spoiling for a fight—probably as her way of putting an end to this situation. But he wasn't about to give it to her, wasn't about to make any of this easy for her after the week of uncertainty he had just suffered through. 'We didn't have sex, Bryn, although we came very close, and, as I said, the location could have been a little more...conventional, but I'm pretty sure there was nothing in the least "weird" about anything we did together.'

Those two wings of colour deepened in her cheeks as she looked up at him with overbright eyes. 'You won't even try to see this from my point of view, will you?'

His jaw tightened. 'I'm not inclined to let you walk away from me just because you *think* your mother might react badly to knowing about the two of us, no.'

'How about if I walk away because *I'm* reacting badly to just the idea of the two of us together?'

His eyes narrowed. 'And are you?'

'Yes!'

'Why?'

She gave an exasperated shake of her head. 'Gabriel, I know you to be an intelligent man—'

'Thank you,' he drawled dryly.

'And as an intelligent man,' she continued firmly, 'you must know how impossible this whole situation is. For goodness' sake, my father went to prison for attempting to defraud you and your family,' she added impatiently when he made no response.

'I'm well aware of what happened five years ago.' He nodded grimly.

'Then you must also be aware— You must have issues of your own about that situation.'

'I deeply regret that I was in the wrong place at the wrong time,' he conceded impatiently. 'But it was sheer coincidence your father chose to bring his painting to Archangel, even more so that I, rather than Michael or Raphael, happened to be in charge of the London gallery when he did.' Something Gabriel had also long had reason to regret.

Except he would never have met Bryn five years ago if not for her father's greed.

She blinked long lashes. 'And you're saying you don't have a problem with that? With the fact that I'm William Harper's daughter?'

'Of course I have a problem with that.' Gabriel swallowed the rest of his wine before placing the empty glass down on the coffee table. 'At the very least it's inconvenient—'

'Inconvenient!' Bryn echoed incredulously.

He nodded. 'Because the past is affecting how you feel about the two of us now.'

Bryn no longer knew how she felt about the past, let alone the here and now.

Five years ago she had been devastated by her father's trial and imprisonment. A month ago she had still been resentful of Gabriel D'Angelo's part in her father's downfall. Even a week ago she had been disgusted with herself for allowing herself to respond to Gabriel in the way that she had.

But Gabriel was asking how she felt about that *now*.

She was still devastated by the events of the past, but the talk she'd had with her mother last week, the things

Mary had told her about the deterioration of her marriage, her daily uncertainty of her own and her daughter's future, how she believed William's get-rich-quick schemes would have eventually caused a complete meltdown in their marriage...

Having spoken with her mother, Bryn now believed that her father, determined to ignore Gabriel's advice to take his painting and just walk away, had instead informed the press of the painting's existence, ballooning the situation beyond anyone's control.

And all of those things put a different slant on that past situation. Bryn had worshipped her father when she was a child, had loved him dearly for the man she had believed him to be. But as an adult she now realised, and was forced to accept, that he had been far from the perfect husband or father.

And, yes, Gabriel had been involved in her father's being sent to prison, but he hadn't done it out of spite, had merely, as he had just pointed out, been caught up in the sequence of events created and executed by Bryn's father, and over which Gabriel himself had no control.

It wasn't the past, or Gabriel's involvement in that past, that made a relationship between the two of them so impossible now; it was how Bryn felt about Gabriel.

Five years ago she had been infatuated, utterly mesmerised, by the dark and devastatingly attractive Gabriel D'Angelo. Since meeting him again, sharing intimacies with him that she had never experienced with any other man, she had realised that it hadn't just been infatuation she had felt for Gabriel five years ago. She had fallen in love with him then, she loved him still, and he—how she felt about him—was why none of the men she had met since had ever held her interest. How could any man compete with Gabriel D'Angelo? Or the fact that Bryn had fallen in love with him all those years ago?

And it was a futile love. Not just because of the past, but because Gabriel, still single at the age of thirty-three, so obviously didn't do falling in love, let alone for ever.

Oh, he was attracted to her, admitted to desiring her, but that was all he felt, and the only way, the only defence Bryn had left against falling even more in love with Gabriel than she already was, was to continue to use the shield of the events of the past to keep him at arm's length.

Gabriel watched through narrowed lids as Bryn swung her feet to the carpeted floor before sitting up.

Her expression was one of cool dismissal. 'I don't feel anything about the two of us now,' she told him coldly.

His jaw tightened. 'That's not—'

'Nor do I think it a good idea for us to be alone together like this again,' she continued firmly. 'You asked that we talk, Gabriel, and we've done that. And I've told you exactly how I feel.' Her chin rose. 'And if anything I've said means you now change your mind about including my paintings in the New Artists Exhibition, then so be it!' she added challengingly as she stood up.

Gabriel eyed her frustratedly, knowing that Bryn was deliberately shutting him out, but he had no idea how to break through the defences she was deliberately putting up against him. The fact that she felt the need to put up those defences at all was surely telling in itself. In what way, Gabriel couldn't be sure. And this stubbornly assertive Bryn obviously wasn't about to enlighten him either.

'I won't change my mind, Bryn,' he assured grimly. 'About anything.' He used the same challenging tone she had to him.

She eyed him guardedly. 'What does that mean?'

Gabriel gave a mocking smile. 'It means that you don't know me very well if you think that anything you've said tonight means I'm going to just walk away from you. It means,' he continued firmly as she would have spoken, 'that, for the two weeks left before the exhibition, I'm going to require that you come to the gallery at least once a day, and that those meetings will be with me, rather than Eric. It means, Bryn, that you can try running away from me, from the attraction between us, but for the next two weeks, at least, I have no intention of allowing you to just ignore me.'

'Why are you doing this?' Tears glistened in those dove-grey eyes.

'Why do you think I'm doing it?' Gabriel rasped, hating being the cause of those tears, but hating even more the idea of giving up on what he knew was between the two of them. Bryn could fight it all she liked, but her responses to him told him that she wanted him as much as he wanted her.

She made a dismissive gesture with her hands. 'Probably because you're the arrogant Gabriel D'Angelo?' she accused huskily. 'Because a D'Angelo doesn't take no for an answer?' She gave a disgusted shake of her head. 'Or possibly because you just enjoy torturing me!'

Gabriel's hands clenched at his sides even as he bared his teeth in a facsimile of a smile. 'Nice try, Bryn, but I've already warned you I'm not backing off because you deliberately insult me.'

'I'm not—'

'Yes, you are, Bryn,' he rasped. 'And yes, I'm arrogant. Enough so that I don't intend taking the answer "no" from the woman I know wants me as much as I want her.'

She drew in a sharp breath.

'You—'

'Your lips might be saying no, Bryn,' he continued remorselessly, 'but the rest of your body, your aroused nipples especially—' he deliberately lowered his gaze to where those hardened nubs were pressed so noticeably against her black cotton shirt '—are definitely saying yes, please!'

Bryn instinctively crossed her arms over her breasts even as she inwardly acknowledged the truth of Gabriel's claim; she *was* aroused from the sensual pleasure of having Gabriel's hands caressing her feet and calves just a few minutes ago, but also because she seemed to be in a constant state of arousal whenever she was in Gabriel's company.

She only had to look at him, into those sultry dark eyes, at those sculptured kissable lips, the long, lean lines of his utterly masculine body, for her own body to become achingly aroused.

And now Gabriel was suggesting—no, ordering—that she spend at least part of every day for the two weeks before the exhibition in his company.

Her eyes glittered with anger now rather than tears. 'I don't even like you very much at this moment, Gabriel.'

He gave another humourless smile as he crossed the distance between them in soft predatory strides. 'If this is not liking me then long may it continue,' he scorned harshly as Bryn took those same steps back, until she could go no farther, her spine pressed flush against the wall as she stared up at him. 'I believe I could become addicted to the way you hate me, Bryn.' Gabriel's expression was grim as he once again held her imprisoned by placing his hands on the wall on either side of her head, his dark gaze deliberately holding hers as his head lowered and his mouth claimed hers.

Bryn groaned low in her throat as, after the briefest hesitation, her arms moved up about Gabriel's shoulders and she met the fierceness of that kiss with a hunger of her own, no room for gentleness as their tongues duelled, Bryn's fingers becoming entangled in the dark thickness of the hair at Gabriel's nape as she moved up on tiptoe to curve her body into his. The softness of her breasts pressed against the hard muscles of Gabriel's chest, her thighs arching as she pressed her mound against the hardness of his arousal, that arousal pulsing in response, growing longer, firmer, as she ground her thighs against his slowly, instinctively seeking that pressure against her hardened nub.

Gabriel wrenched his mouth from hers to hungrily kiss the length of her throat, the tops of her breasts, groaning his frustration as her fastened shirt stopped him from going any lower. A barrier he easily dispensed with by taking hold of both sides of her shirt and simply pulling, several buttons flying off as he pushed the shirt down her arms and let it fall to the floor.

'Oh, yes,' he rasped hotly as he gazed down hungrily at the creamy swell of her breasts visible above a red lace bra. 'I'm going to lick and suck your oh-so-sensitive breasts—' his gaze held hers as one of his hands moved to unfasten the clasp at the back of her bra before dropping it down onto the floor with her shirt '—and I'm going to continue licking, sucking and biting these pretty breasts—' his hands moved up to cup those thrusting globes tipped by swollen strawberry-ripe nipples '—until you come for me again.'

Bryn felt her cheeks pale. 'No, Gabriel—'

'Yes, Bryn,' he ground out harshly, eyes feverish, his skin flushed against the hard blades of his cheekbones. 'You want it as much as I do.'

She did. Oh, yes, she most certainly did. She ached to feel Gabriel's lips and hands on her again, and that amazing, overwhelming feeling when he brought her to climax.

'These are mine, Bryn.' Gabriel's hands squeezed her breasts. 'Do you understand? These are all mine. To lick and suck, to give you pleasure! And I'm not letting you walk out of here tonight until I've proven that to you!' The past few minutes—Bryn's rejection of there ever being a relationship between the two of them, of Gabriel himself—seemed to have stripped him of showing even a veneer of civilised behaviour.

A loss of control that had touched an equally primitive need deep inside Bryn.

Heat gushed between her thighs, the nubbin swelling, pulsing, in the dampness of her curls as Gabriel lowered his head and sucked one nipple deep into the heat of his mouth even as the thumb and finger of his other hand captured and plucked its twin into the same throbbing needing.

Again and again he suckled her nipple, remorselessly caressing and squeezing its twin, both just short of pain, until Bryn was wild, mindless with hunger, with a need that pulsed and ached between her thighs and caused her to groan, to arch her spine, forcing her breast even deeper into the tormenting heat of Gabriel's mouth as he pressed his thigh rhythmically against that swollen nubbin.

'Gabriel?' Bryn gasped in protest as he released her breast to look up at her.

'Come for me, Bryn,' he encouraged throatily. 'Watch me as I take you over the edge. No way, Bryn!' he refused fiercely as she used the last slender thread of her control to defy him by turning her head away. 'Do you want me to stop?' he rasped harshly. 'Look at me now, Bryn, and tell me you want me to stop!'

A sob caught in her throat as she slowly turned back to him, instantly losing herself in the glittering black pools of his feverish gaze.

'Tell me to stop, Bryn, and I will,' he encouraged huskily.

'I—I can't,' she sobbed. 'Don't stop, Gabriel!' she urged achingly as her fingers tightened in his hair, drawing him back towards her breasts. 'Please don't stop!'

'Look at me this time, Bryn,' he encouraged softly, his breath a warm caress across the aching moistness of her swollen nipple. 'I want to look into your eyes as you come for me.' His tongue flicked out, a tormenting lash against her swollen and aching nipple, continuing to rasp that tongue against her, his gaze continuing to hold hers as he released the button of her jeans before sliding the zip slowly down.

Bryn couldn't have looked away if she had tried, her pleasure swelling, rising out of control, at the eroticism of watching Gabriel as he now parted his lips about her nipple before suckling, gently at first, and then more deeply, her breathing hitching, fracturing as she felt his hand against the heat of her abdomen as it slid beneath the red lace of her panties, his fingers lightly circling her swollen nubbin.

Again and again those tormenting fingers stroked, above and then below that swollen nubbin, dipping his fingers into the dampness of her channel before slowly caressing but never quite touching her right where she most craved his touch, never giving her the pressure there that she ached for.

'Please, Gabriel,' Bryn gasped when she couldn't bear the torment a moment longer. 'Please! Oh, yes,' she gasped, her hands clinging to his shoulders, her thighs thrusting up instinctively as his fingers finally brushed lightly over that aching nubbin. 'Harder, Gabriel! Harder!' She cried out as the pleasure built, higher and then higher still as he increased the pressure and speed of his stroking fingers.

'Let go, Bryn,' Gabriel encouraged harshly against the creaminess of her breast. 'Come for me.' He captured the swollen nubbin between his fingers, squeezing as his mouth returned to her breast, drawing greedily on her nipple as he felt that nubbin throb and then pulse between his fingers as Bryn shattered into a shuddering, gasping climax, as he took it all, unwilling, unable to stop, until he had wrung out every last shuddering, trembling ounce of her orgasm.

'Oh, God, oh, God, oh, God!' Her head dropped down weakly onto Gabriel's shoulder as she continued to quiver and shake and cling to him in the aftermath of her pleasure.

Gabriel took her into his arms and held her tightly against his chest, his breathing as ragged and uneven as hers. 'And that, my beautiful Bryn, is why I refuse to walk away from you. From this. From us,' he told her gruffly. 'Not even if you beg me to.'

Bryn wanted to beg, not for Gabriel to walk away, but for him to continue making love to her.

Again and again.

Which was why *she* had to walk away.

CHAPTER TEN

THE NEXT TWO weeks were absolute hell for Bryn, compelled, as Gabriel had promised she would be, to go to Archangel and see him on a daily basis as they dealt with putting the final details of the exhibition into place.

Not that he ever attempted, or even indicated he wished, to repeat the intimacy of that night at his apartment. Oh, no, Gabriel had a much more subtle torment than that, as he took every opportunity to touch her, always seemingly accidentally: brushing lightly against her to emphasise a point, placing his hand on hers, or at the sensitive base of her spine, or the glide of her hips, whenever the opportunity arose.

And he did it all without saying a word or showing outward acknowledgement of the attraction that sparked and burned between the two of them every time they were together.

Bryn quickly realised that Gabriel really was intent on torturing her.

And how well he was succeeding.

As day followed torturous day Bryn's awareness of Gabriel grew to such a degree that she began to tremble and shake even as she approached the Archangel Gallery. Her nerves would be strung tightly, her body tingling with awareness, as she wondered if that would be the day Gabriel would relent and kiss her, caress her, before she went quietly insane with this growing need for him.

By the day of the exhibition Bryn knew she had never been so aware of a man in her life: his smell—that seductive male smell, a spicy musk, that was uniquely Gabriel—the rippling play of muscles across his shoulders and back when he removed his jacket and tie. He'd unfasten the top two buttons of his shirt to reveal a light dusting of dark hair on his chest whenever they weren't in the public galleries, allowing her to fully appreciate that masculinity. Her fingers literally itched to become entangled in the glossy dark hair she could see on his chest, to caress the firm line of his back, the silky hair at his nape.

She only had to get through one more day, just a few more hours of this torture, Bryn told herself on that final morning as she made her way to Archangel and the closed west gallery, where the paintings of the six artists were finally ready to be exhibited at a private invitation-only showing this evening.

Unfortunately, Bryn realised as she came to an abrupt halt in the doorway to the west gallery, today was going to be the most difficult twenty-four hours of the past two weeks of torture. Her breath caught in her throat and her face paled as she saw, and easily recognised, the three men talking quietly together across the room.

Gabriel was instantly recognisable, of course, but the unmistakable likeness between all three men—tall and lean, dark haired, with hewn and handsome olive-skinned faces—told her that the other two men had to be Gabriel's two brothers, Michael and Raphael D'Angelo.

Two men who had absolutely no reason to feel in the least kindly towards Sabryna Harper.

* * *

Gabriel sensed Bryn's presence in the gallery even before he turned and saw her standing pale and still across the room; his senses had become so heightened to her presence during these past two weeks that he now felt a thrum of awareness beneath the surface of his skin whenever she was anywhere near. His shaft would harden, becoming a painful throb just at the smell of her perfume— that exotic spice, and the womanly smell that he knew was all uniquely aroused Bryn—the husky sound of her voice enough to raise the hairs on the back of his neck and send shivers of pleasure down the length of his spine.

Gabriel had lost count of the amount of times he had been tempted to put an end to the torment that made his days a living hell and his nights a sleepless nightmare, to just take Bryn in his arms and make love to her, to keep her there until she admitted she wanted him with the same fierce hunger that he wanted her.

The only thing that held him back from doing that was Bryn herself.

For both their sakes she had to be the one to come to him this time. Through her own choice, and not because of any physical coercion on his part. And if that required that he go quietly out of his mind while he waited— hoped—for that to happen, then so be it!

The fact that Bryn looked small and vulnerable today in a dark grey blouse and black jeans, her eyes apprehensive as she stared across the gallery at the three of them, was enough to tell him that she had found the past two weeks as much of a strain as he had.

'Bryn?' he prompted gently as she made no effort to come farther into the gallery.

Her chin rose. 'I— Excuse me, I just wanted— I didn't realise there was anyone— I'll come back later,' she muttered awkwardly as she turned away with the obvious intention of hurrying from the gallery. And maybe Archangel itself?

'Bryn!' Gabriel called out harshly.

She came to an abrupt halt, her tension visible in the stiffness of her shoulders and spine, her hands clenching and unclenching at her sides as she obviously debated whether or not she was going to turn back and face him or simply continue running.

Gabriel mentally willed her to do the former rather than the latter, to be that strong and confident Bryn that he so admired as well as desired.

Bryn felt slightly light-headed as she forgot to breathe, her heart beating so loud and wildly in her chest that she felt sure the three men standing across the room must be able to hear it.

She hadn't known—hadn't even guessed. No one had thought to warn her—certainly not Gabriel—that his brothers were going to be in London today. For the purpose of attending the exhibition this evening?

Wasn't it bad enough that she had been forced to deal with Gabriel on a daily basis for the past two weeks, that her nerves were shot to hell because of it, without having to now face his two disapproving brothers?

Except there was no escaping the fact that Michael and Raphael D'Angelo were both here, that they were the co-owners of the Archangel Galleries, and as such Bryn knew she had no choice but to face them at some point today. So perhaps it was better if she did so sooner rather than in public later, when the meeting could be even more embarrassing?

Bryn drew in a ragged, steadying breath before turning slowly, her chin tilting defensively as she kept her gaze fixed firmly on Gabriel rather than looking at either of his two brothers. 'I was just—' She moistened the dryness of her lips with the tip of her tongue. 'I thought I would come and take a last look in here before the exhibition this evening.'

'I'm glad you did.' Gabriel nodded, dark eyes hooded, his expression unreadable as he crossed the room in long graceful strides to stand in front of her. 'My brothers would like to meet you,' he encouraged gruffly.

Bryn barely managed to hold back her snort of derision as she looked up at him sceptically; they both knew she was the last person Michael and Raphael D'Angelo would ever wish to be introduced to. 'I thought your brothers didn't approve of my inclusion in the exhibition?' she said loud enough for all three men to hear.

Gabriel's jaw tightened at the directness of her challenge, his gaze dark and disapproving as he frowned down at her.

'We initially questioned your motives for entering the New Artists competition, yes,' one of the two men across the room—Michael or Raphael?—came back just as directly.

'Shut up, Rafe,' Gabriel rasped dismissively.

'Some of us still do.' Raphael ignored him as he strolled across the gallery, dark sable hair long and curling silkily onto his shoulders, more casually dressed than his two brothers in a tight black T-shirt that emphasised the muscled width of his shoulders and chest, faded denims resting low down on the leanness of his hips, heavy black boots on his feet. 'I don't believe Gabriel has bothered to ask you this, but why us and why here, Miss Jones?' He quirked a dark and mocking brow.

'Shut up, Rafe,' the third man instructed harshly—he had to be Michael D'Angelo—as he crossed the room with more forceful strides, his sable hair cropped close to his head, his eyes so dark a brown they appeared black and unfathomable, a three-piece charcoal-grey suit perfectly tailored to his muscular frame, his shirt the palest grey, a darker grey silk tie neatly knotted at his throat. 'I'm Michael D'Angelo, Miss Jones.' His tone was compelling as he held his hand out to her.

Bryn eyed that hand uncertainly even as she felt the compulsion in that voice, enough so that she ran the dampness of her own hand down her denim-clad thighs before raising it to be clasped firmly, briefly, in Michael D'Angelo's much stronger one before he released her again. 'I believe we all know that my name isn't really Jones,' she murmured.

'Confrontational. I like that,' Raphael D'Angelo drawled encouragingly.

'Shut up, Rafe.' Gabriel and Michael spoke together this time, both their tones weary, as if they had suffered years of repeating that same phrase.

Bryn bit her lip uncertainly as she quickly looked at each of the three D'Angelo brothers in turn: Gabriel glowered at Rafe impatiently, Michael also frowned at his sibling while Rafe grinned unrepentantly at both of them before turning to give Bryn a conspiratorial wink.

Her eyes widened as she realised Rafe D'Angelo, rather than seriously challengingly her, was, in fact, deliberately annoying his two brothers.

'I don't understand any of this.' She gave a dazed shake of her head.

'Not even Gabriel?' Raphael came back speculatively.

'Rafe—'

'I know, shut up.' Raphael lightly acknowledged Gabriel's rebuke as he pushed his hands into the front pockets of his denims. 'I don't know why it is, but you and Michael just love to ruin all my fun.' He shrugged.

Bryn really was baffled by Michael and Raphael D'Angelo; she had expected hostility, at least, from the two of them because of who she was and the damage her father could have caused the Archangel Galleries five years ago. A hostility that she realised simply wasn't there.

Admittedly Michael was a little austere, self-contained, restrained, in both appearance and manner, but that seemed to be his normal demeanour, rather than any personal animosity directed towards her.

As for Raphael... Bryn had a feeling, looking into those predatory and shrewd golden eyes, that Rafe D'Angelo was a man who maintained a wickedly irreverent appearance on the outside as a way of keeping his real feelings very close to that beautifully muscled chest.

Gabriel easily saw the bewilderment in Bryn's expression as she looked at his two brothers.

Just as he recognised Rafe's open appreciation for Bryn as he mockingly returned that curious gaze. An appreciation that Gabriel didn't like in the least, following his own two weeks of private hell as he had forced himself not to touch or kiss Bryn.

He put a proprietary hand beneath Bryn's elbow now as he stepped closer to her. 'If the two of you will excuse us, I want to talk to Bryn upstairs in my office for a few minutes.'

'"Talk" to her, Gabriel?' Rafe came back derisively.

He gave his brother a narrow-eyed look of warning. 'I'll see the two of you later this evening.'

'You can count on it,' Rafe came back challengingly. 'I'm very much looking forward to seeing you again this evening, Bryn,' he added huskily.

'For God's sake, Rafe, will you just—?'

'I know, I know. Shut up,' Rafe sighed heavily at Michael's terse admonishment.

Gabriel gave a shake of his head as he and Bryn finally left the gallery together, maintaining his hold on her elbow as the two of them walked towards the private lift at the end of the marble hallway. 'I apologise for Rafe,' he bit out abruptly. 'As you may have gathered, he has a warped sense of humour.' A warped sense of humour that on this occasion had been at Gabriel's expense; Rafe knew and had played upon the fact that Gabriel hadn't liked the interest he had shown in Bryn.

'He seemed…very nice,' Bryn answered him uncertainly as they stepped into the lift together.

'Nice is not a word I would ever use to describe my brother,' Gabriel rasped. 'Annoying, irritating, sometimes infuriating, but never anything as insipid as "nice".' Even as he said it Gabriel knew he was being unfair to Rafe; after all, his brother had been the one to warn him that Bryn Jones was Sabryna Harper after Michael had decided against doing so.

'Both your brothers were far more polite to me than I could ever have expected, in the circumstances,' she murmured softly as they stepped out of the lift and walked down the hallway to Gabriel's office.

Gabriel shot her a sideways glance. 'Than I led you to believe, perhaps?'

'Well… Yes.'

He drew in a sharp breath at the speculation in Bryn's tone. 'I advise you not to complicate an already impossible situation by falling for the charms of one of my brothers!' he bit out harshly.

'I wasn't— I didn't— Why would you even think I might do that?' Bryn reacted with predictable accusation.

'You already know the answer to that question, Bryn,'

Gabriel murmured as they entered his office, closing the door firmly behind them before turning Bryn in his arms, his hands resting lightly on the slenderness of her hips.

'Do I?'

'Yes.' He nodded. 'But just so that there's no misunderstanding—if any of the D'Angelo bothers is going to be allowed to kiss these delectable lips today, then it's going to be me,' Gabriel assured her gruffly as he raised one of his hands to run a fingertip gently over her fuller, sensuous bottom lip.

Her eyes darkened, cheeks suffusing with colour. 'I'm not interested in being kissed by either Raphael or Michael,' she breathed softly.

'I'm glad to hear it.' Gabriel's hand moved beneath her chin and tilted her face up towards his, his other arm moving lightly about her waist as he moulded the softness of her curves against his much harder ones. 'How about me, Bryn? Are you interested in kissing me?'

'Gabriel…' she groaned breathily.

It took every particle of willpower Gabriel possessed not to just take that kiss as he felt the way Bryn's body trembled against his, but he knew that he couldn't, wanting, needing Bryn to make the first move. 'A single kiss, Bryn,' he encouraged throatily. 'For luck. To the success of the exhibition this evening.' His breath caught in his throat as he waited for her answer.

Bryn gazed up at him searchingly, longing, aching to once again feel Gabriel's lips on hers, to lose herself in that pleasure. At the same time as she knew that a single kiss wouldn't be enough, that she wanted so much more from Gabriel than just passion and pleasure. So very much more. And that Gabriel didn't have any more than that to give her.

'I can't,' she breathed softly as she pushed against his chest to be released.

Something dark and primal moved in the depths of his eyes as his arms tightened about her. 'Can't or won't, Bryn?' he rasped harshly.

She closed her eyes briefly before answering him. 'Let me go, Gabriel.'

His mouth thinned, a nerve pulsing in the tightness of his jaw. 'Why are you doing this, Bryn?' he groaned. 'Why are you making us both suffer because of your stubbornness?'

This wasn't about Bryn being stubborn; it was so much more than that—*she* felt so much more than that. 'You know why.'

'Because you're worried about your mother,' Gabriel rasped. 'Because of how you believe she would feel about the two of us being together.'

Tears burned in her eyes. 'And you don't think that's important?' she choked. 'You believe that I should just take what I want and to hell with how it affects anyone else?'

'If I'm what you want, then, yes, damn it, that's exactly what I think you should do!' His eyes glittered darkly.

Bryn gave a shake of her head. 'You said it yourself, Gabriel. This is an impossible situation that doesn't need to be made any more complicated than it already is.'

'And when I said it I was warning you not to take Rafe's flirtation seriously,' he grated harshly.

Bryn blinked back the heat of tears. 'Gabriel, we only have one last day together to get through. Do you think we could try to do that without arguing?'

His expression sharpened. 'You think I'm just going to gracefully bow out of your life after tonight?'

She tensed. 'I was under the impression— Eric told me weeks ago that you would be returning to the Paris gallery after the opening night of the New Artists Exhibition.'

'Did he?' Gabriel gave a humourless smile.

Bryn looked up at him searchingly, a sick feeling forming in the pit of her stomach as he met her gaze unblinkingly. 'You don't intend going back to Paris tomorrow?' she guessed weakly.

'No, I don't,' he answered with satisfaction. 'In fact, Rafe, Michael and I were discussing that very thing when you arrived. Michael is flying to New York tomorrow to take over the gallery there for a month, Rafe is going to Archangel in Paris and I'm staying right here to oversee the rest of the New Artists Exhibition and auction.'

And Bryn knew that the exhibition was being opened to the public tomorrow, the paintings to be on display until they were included in the next Archangel auction in two weeks' time.

Which meant that Gabriel was going to be in London for at least those same two weeks, possibly longer— and his very presence in London would continue to be such a torment and torture that she wouldn't know a moment's peace.

'Let me go, Gabriel,' she instructed. 'Please,' she added as his arms remained firmly about her waist. 'I have to be at the coffee shop by ten o'clock.'

He frowned darkly as he slowly released her. 'You're working today?'

'Of course I'm working today,' she dismissed impatiently as she stepped away from him, finally able to breathe again now that she wasn't pressed up against the disturbing length of his body. 'I haven't sold any of my paintings yet, and I still have my rent to pay at the end of the month,' she added ruefully.

Gabriel moved to lean back against the front of his desk. 'As of this morning, one of your paintings has a reserved sticker on it.'

Her gaze sharpened. 'It does?'

Gabriel nodded. 'Michael wants it.'

Her eyes widened. 'He does?'

Gabriel smiled ruefully. 'Hmm.'

'Which one?'

'The rose.'

The dying red rose, Bryn's representation of the death of hopes and dreams rather than just the flower itself.

Did the austere Michael D'Angelo, a man who gave the appearance of being so totally self-contained, a man who surely had no hopes and dreams to die, appreciate the full meaning of her painting?

'That's— I'm flattered,' Bryn murmured softly.

Gabriel nodded grimly. 'You should be. Michael's private art collection is very exclusive. I have every reason to believe that Lord Simmons is very interested in purchasing one too.'

'That's...amazing.' Bryn's eyes glowed excitedly as she reached out and grasped his hands impulsively. 'This is really going to happen, isn't it, Gabriel? I'm really going to sell some of my paintings, maybe even be able to paint full-time!'

'It's as real as it gets, yes,' Gabriel confirmed huskily as he pulled her in between his parted thighs before placing her hands against his chest. 'Tonight is your night, Bryn.' His hands cupped either side of her face as he gave in to the hunger and kissed her gently on the lips that had haunted and tormented him for the past five years. 'And I want you to enjoy it. Every single moment of it,' he encouraged.

'Oh, I will,' she assured him happily, her hands warm against his chest. 'I— Thank you, Gabriel, for giving me this chance. I really— I know I've been difficult on occasion—' she grimaced '—but I—I really do appreciate everything you've done for me.'

Gabriel could only hope that Bryn still felt that way after tonight.

The past two weeks of being close to Bryn, but never quite close enough, had been enough of a hell for Gabriel to know that the two of them couldn't go on like this indefinitely, that something had to change, and that it wasn't going to be the way he felt about Bryn.

So he had made his arrangements accordingly. Carefully and quietly. Arrangements that would come to full fruition later this evening.

And he wasn't sure Bryn would ever forgive him.

CHAPTER ELEVEN

'IS IT EVERYTHING you hoped it would be?'

Bryn turned to smile warmly at Eric as he came to stand beside her. 'It's so much more!' Her smile widened as he handed her one of the glasses of champagne he carried.

There were over two hundred people crowded into the west gallery for this invitation-only showing, the men all wearing evening suits, the women chic and glittering in their evening gowns and expensive jewellery. Two dozen waiters circulated amongst them carrying trays of finger food and glasses of champagne and half a dozen huge arrangements of flowers perfumed the brightly lit room, all adding to Bryn's light-headed euphoria.

Bryn had chosen to wear a simple black sheath of an above-the-knee length, her only jewellery a simple silver bracelet about one of her wrists and a silver locket at her throat, both of them presents from her mother.

Her smile faded a little at thoughts of her mother, knowing how much Mary would have loved all of this, how proud she would have been of Bryn's success. Instead, Bryn still hadn't so much as dared to tell her mother about the exhibition; how could she when that exhibition was being held at the Archangel Gallery?

As might be expected, the D'Angelo brothers all

looked amazingly handsome in their evening suits as they stood head, and sometimes shoulders, above the other guests, the darkness of their different lengths of hair becoming a sable sheen below the glittering lights of the chandeliers above them. Michael was as remotely austere as ever when he gave her a brief nod of acknowledgement earlier, Rafe as rakishly devil-may-care as he shot her another wink.

But to Bryn's biased gaze Gabriel was far and away the most distinguished man in the room, and she once again found her gaze shifting to the other side of the gallery where he stood in conversation with David Simmons. His mesmerising and dark good looks drew Bryn's gaze to him again and again as if pulled by a magnet, her heart now skipping a beat as Gabriel laughed easily at something the older man had just said to him.

A heart that ached. To be with Gabriel. To make love with him, just once.

Gabriel stilled as he felt a prickle of awareness, of being watched, at his nape and down his spine. Allowing his gaze to move unhurriedly about the room, he sought the source of that awareness even as he continued his conversation with the enthusiastic David Simmons.

Bryn.

Standing beside Eric on the other side of the crowded gallery, her eyes a deep and misty grey as they looked directly into his, the fullness of her lips curving into an enigmatic smile.

Gabriel raised his champagne glass to her in a silent toast; the exhibition was only an hour old but already Bryn's paintings were noticeably attracting the most attention.

Her smile widened as she accepted his silent toast, her eyes glowing. With happiness? Or something else?

'—keep you any longer when I can see I'm keeping you from where you really want to be,' David drawled dryly.

Gabriel drew his gaze reluctantly from Bryn's as he turned back to the other man. 'Sorry?'

The older man chuckled good-naturedly. 'I advise you go to her, man!'

Gabriel gave a rueful smile. 'Is it that obvious?'

David continued to smile indulgently. 'Lovely-looking girl. Beautiful as well as talented. Deadly combination, hmm?'

'Deadly,' Gabriel accepted heavily.

'Then go to it, man.' David gave him an encouraging slap on the shoulder. 'Before that rascal of a brother of yours beats you to it,' he added with a pointed look at Rafe making his way determinedly in Bryn's direction.

'Damn you, Rafe,' Gabriel muttered impatiently even as he placed his empty champagne glass on the tray of one of the passing waiters before striding forcefully across the room to intercept his brother. 'This isn't what we agreed your role would be this evening, Rafe!' He glowered in warning.

Rafe raised mocking brows. 'I just thought I would keep Bryn company while I'm waiting. She looks absolutely stunning this evening, by the way.'

'Hands off, Rafe,' he growled.

His brother grinned unrepentantly. 'Does Bryn know how damned possessive you are over her?'

'Yes.' He frowned grimly, not sure that Bryn wasn't actually going to hate him by the end of this evening.

Rafe chuckled. 'And have you told her how you feel about her yet?'

'Go to hell, Rafe.'

Rafe looked comfortably unconcerned. 'Of course. Why do things the easy way when you can so easily complicate the hell out of them?' He gave a rueful shake of his head. 'At this rate you're going to end up as cold and remote as Michael!'

Gabriel glanced across to where their older brother managed to remain withdrawn even while mingling with their guests. 'He likes his life that way.' He shrugged.

'But you don't, not anymore. Which is why——' Rafe turned back to Gabriel, brows raised '——complicated or not, you should just grab your woman and to hell with everything else!'

'We both know it isn't that simple where Bryn is concerned.' Gabriel grimaced.

'Then I suggest you make it that simple and put the rest of us out of our misery.'

'Your turn will come, Rafe,' Gabriel warned impatiently. 'And when it does we'll see just how well you deal with it. And her.'

Rafe gave a scornful snort. 'There isn't a snowball's chance in hell that I'm going to let some woman—any woman!—come between me and my bachelor lifestyle.'

'Oh, it will come, Rafe, take my word for it, and when it does I'm going to enjoy seeing you have to eat your words.' Gabriel chuckled with satisfaction. 'In the meantime, keep your lethal charms away from Bryn,' he added firmly.

'Just can't stand the competition, hmm?'

'You're too irritating for me to consider you serious competition,' Gabriel drawled dismissively, his gaze once again returning to, and remaining on, Bryn as she chatted with Eric. 'If you'll excuse me, I think I'll go and talk to "my woman".' But before he could even begin to cross the room to Bryn's side he saw her face pale, her eyes widening in distress as she stared across at the entrance to the gallery.

And Gabriel knew, without needing to turn and look, that the moment of truth had arrived.

'Go now, Rafe!' he rasped harshly as he strode towards Bryn.

Bryn was sure she had to be hallucinating, brought about, no doubt, by the strain of the past two weeks and too much champagne on an empty stomach; she had been too excited about this evening to even think about eating today!

Because she couldn't really be looking at her mother and Rhys standing in the entrance to the gallery; it had to be her guilty thoughts of a few minutes ago that made her imagine she could.

Except… Bryn was sure she would never have imagined Rhys looking so handsome in an evening suit; as far as she was aware her stepfather didn't even own an evening suit. In fact, she didn't think she had ever seen Rhys in anything other than jeans and casual tops, T-shirts or sweaters, depending on the time of year. He had worn a suit at his wedding with Mary, of course, but as far as Bryn knew that had been put at the back of his wardrobe the day after the wedding and forgotten about.

Her mother looked slender and beautiful, of course, in her favourite gown, the same deep grey as her eyes, her ivory skin flawless, pale peach lip gloss on her parted lips.

A smile now curved those peach-coloured lips, grey eyes lighting up with excitement, as Mary looked straight across at Bryn before her attention was distracted by Raphael D'Angelo as he joined them in the doorway, speaking briefly before kissing Mary's hand and shaking Rhys's.

Bryn knew there was no way she could have imagined that.

Which meant her mother and Rhys really were here. How on earth had—?

Gabriel!

Gabriel had to have done this.

But why?

Why would Gabriel do something so potentially destructive to what should have been a glitteringly successful evening for the Archangel Gallery? Was he, despite having consistently denied it, still so absorbed in the past that he was willing to take his revenge against Mary and Bryn at the cost of that success and all the weeks of hard work that had gone into this exhibition?

No.

Bryn couldn't believe that of him. She *wouldn't* believe that of the man she loved and had come to know so well these past few weeks. There had to be another reason, an innocent reason, for Gabriel having deliberately invited her mother and Rhys to the exhibition.

'Bryn? Bryn!'

She turned sharply at the sound of Gabriel's voice, trying to focus through the black spots wavering in front of her eyes. 'Why?' she had time to gasp before those black spots all merged into one huge black hole into which Bryn thankfully fell.

She wasn't aware of being swept up into Gabriel's arms, of the sympathetic gasps of the other guests as he carried her across the room, or her mother's concern as she followed the two of them out of the gallery and up to Gabriel's office, leaving her stepfather and Rafe to deal with providing an explanation for her having fainted.

No, Bryn was aware of none of that as she slowly returned to consciousness and heard her mother and Gabriel talking softly together.

'——should have warned her,' Gabriel muttered disgustedly, holding Bryn's hand tightly in his as he sat beside her limp form on the sofa in his office.

'You wanted it to be a surprise,' Mary soothed.

'And this is the result!' he cursed grimly as he looked down at Bryn, her lashes very dark against the pale delicacy of her face.

'It's just a faint, Gabriel,' Bryn's mother assured ruefully. 'If I know my little girl, she's been too excited about tonight to bother eating today.'

Gabriel stood up abruptly, running an agitated hand through the dark thickness of his hair. 'I just wanted her to have the two of you here tonight to share in her success.'

'I know that, Gabriel,' Mary assured gently. 'And so will Bryn once she's thought things through.'

'You think?' Gabriel knew Bryn well enough by now—knew what she thought of him only too well—to know that she was more than capable of believing he had some Machiavellian reason for inviting her mother and stepfather to the exhibition.

Because he hadn't thought his actions through properly, should have realised the shock it would be for Bryn when Mary and Rhys arrived at the gallery this evening.

'I think,' Mary echoed, having now taken Gabriel's place on the sofa beside Bryn. 'I accept my daughter can be fiery on occasion, Gabriel—part of her Welsh heritage, I'm afraid,' she added ruefully. 'But she isn't so headstrong that she will judge you unfairly. And what you've done for her, in regard to her inclusion in this exhibition at Archangel, and inviting Rhys and I here this evening to share in her success, was incredibly kind of you.'

'Bryn doesn't see me as being in the least kind,' Gabriel drawled ruefully.

'Oh, I think you might be pleasantly surprised at what my daughter sees in you,' Mary murmured dryly.

Bryn knew that last remark was directed towards her rather than Gabriel, that her mother, at least, was aware Bryn had recovered from her faint but was now choosing to appear as if she hadn't.

Mary squeezed her hand to confirm it. 'When she wakes up you need to tell Bryn everything, Gabriel,' she told him—and Bryn—softly. 'She especially needs to know what you did for us five years ago, what you did to help the two of us make a new life together in Wales after William died.'

Bryn frowned at this revelation, at the same time knowing her mother's comment 'when she wakes up' was pointedly directed at her.

And she did need to do that; lying here listening to this conversation was totally unfair to Gabriel. Besides, she very much wanted to hear all about what Gabriel had done for them five years ago.

Mary released Bryn's hand before standing up. 'You're a good man, Gabriel,' she told him. 'And if you give my daughter a chance, I believe you will find she already knows that. Now, I think it's time I returned back downstairs, and left the two of you alone to talk.'

'But—'

'My mother is right, Gabriel,' Bryn spoke at the same time as she opened her eyes and looked up at them both. 'You and I do need to talk.' She swung her legs to the floor and sat up slowly.

'I'm not sure you should do that just yet.' Gabriel stepped swiftly forward and sat down on the sofa beside her before once again taking one of her hands in both of his. 'You're probably a bit shaky still from—'

'Mamma?' Bryn looked up at her mother pointedly.

Mary nodded. 'I'm going downstairs now to bask in some of my daughter's glory,' she murmured indulgently. 'No doubt I will see the two of you sometime later this evening?'

'No doubt,' Bryn nodded distractedly, having eyes only for Gabriel.

'And, Bryn?' Her mother paused in the doorway. 'You're wrong. Gabriel isn't in the least "unsuitable". In any way,' she assured before she left the office and closed the door softly behind her.

CHAPTER TWELVE

'WHAT WAS THAT about?' Gabriel prompted.

Bryn's vision was slightly misty with tears as she turned to look at him, knowing that her mother had been referring to the conversation the two of them had had in Wales three weeks ago, when Bryn had insisted the man she loved wasn't suitable.

She gave a shake of her head. 'It doesn't matter anymore. I— Gabriel, I need to thank you for inviting my mother and Rhys here tonight. It's made my evening so much more special.'

'So much so you fainted, damn it,' Gabriel grated self-disgustedly.

Bryn held on to his hand as he would have pulled away and stood up. 'I want you to stay right here,' she told him firmly as he looked at her questioningly. 'I need to say some things to you, and I want you to be next to me when I say them.'

A frown appeared between his eyes. 'Am I going to need some of my single-malt whisky to get through this?' he drawled.

'I don't believe so, no.' She smiled ruefully, drawing in a deep breath before speaking again. 'I'll admit, when I first realised my mother and Rhys were really here—rather than just a figment of my food-deprived, champagne-induced imagination—that I wondered why you had done it. I only wondered for the briefest of moments, Gabriel,' she assured as his frown darkened. 'The very briefest of moments,' she repeated firmly, 'before my knowledge of you told me that your reason for doing it would be a good one rather than a bad one.'

'Actually, it was purely selfish.' Gabriel grimaced; he wanted this woman so badly he was willing to do anything—anything—to get her.

Bryn gave a firm shake of her head. 'I don't believe that.'

'Oh, but it was. You kept insisting that there could never be anything between the two of us because of how your mother might react if she knew, and so I decided to eliminate that objection, at least.'

Bryn looked at him searchingly for several long seconds before a slow smile curved her lips. 'I accept that might have been one of the reasons, Gabriel—'

'Oh, believe me, it was the prime reason,' he assured her grimly.

Her smile didn't even waver. 'You like people to think you're tough and uncaring, don't you?'

'I am tough and—'

'You are most certainly not uncaring,' she insisted firmly. 'And you may manage to convince other people that you are, but I think you should know I haven't fallen for it for some time now. Not since I realised I was in love with you,' she added softly.

'Bryn?' Gabriel's hand tightened about hers.

'Don't worry, I'm not saying that with any expectation of you returning the sentiment,' she assured ruefully. 'I just think you should know, before we start our affair, that I've realised since meeting you again that I fell in love with you five years ago—'

'You— What affair?' Gabriel demanded sharply as he released her hand before standing up.

'—and that I'm still in love with you,' Bryn continued determinedly. 'And that I have no intention of having any sort of relationship with you now and pretending that I'm not—'

'Bryn, did you really just say you fell in love with me five years ago?' he repeated dazedly.

'I did, yes,' she admitted wryly. 'And the reason I'm telling you this now is because I want you to know how I feel before you tell me in what way you helped my mother and I five years ago. It's time for us to be honest with each other, Gabriel,' she encouraged softly. 'As such, I don't want there to be any misunderstandings about why and when I fell in love with you.'

His eyes widened. 'You heard your mother and I talking just now?'

'Yes.'

Gabriel looked down at her searchingly, Bryn meeting that searching gaze unwaveringly. 'You really fell in love with me five years ago?' he finally murmured.

Bryn nodded. 'On sight, I think. But it was all such a mess after my father was arrested. At the time I wondered how I could possibly still be in love with the man who had helped to put my father in prison,' she added heavily. 'I know the truth about that now, Gabriel,' she assured him firmly. 'I know that you tried to stop him, to save him from himself, and my father's answer to that was to inform the press, and so making it impossible for him to walk away as you wanted him to do. I do believe that, Gabriel.'

'Thank God,' he groaned with feeling. 'You really love me, Bryn?' He looked at her searchingly.

She nodded. 'In fact, I realised a couple weeks ago that you're the reason I'm still a virgin at the grand old age of twenty-three,' she acknowledged self-derisively. 'No other man quite matched up to my first love.' She looked up at Gabriel uncertainly as he still looked stunned. 'Too much honesty for you?'

Too much? It was perfect as far as Gabriel was concerned. Bryn was perfect. For him. She always had been.

'I have no words to tell you how much it…pleased me, to know there's been no one else for you.' Gabriel gave a rueful shake of his head. 'But you should know now that I don't want to have an affair with you.'

She blinked. 'Okay.' She nodded woodenly. 'More fool me for having believed you still did.' She drew in a deep, steadying breath. 'That makes all of this a little embarrassing, but it doesn't change any of what I've said—'

'Bryn, would it surprise you to know that I fell in love with you five years ago too?'

She stilled, staring up at him with wide eyes, a gaze that Gabriel now returned with the same directness as she had a few minutes ago. 'I know you said something like this before but—you couldn't have done,' she finally managed to protest dismissively. 'I was chubby,' she reminded him. 'I wore those unbecoming dark-framed glasses. I was so ungainly I fell over my own feet all the time—' She broke off as Gabriel gave a slow shake of his head.

'To me you were voluptuously sexy,' he corrected firmly. 'And you had—still have—the most beautiful dove-grey eyes I've ever seen, glasses or no glasses. I found your occasional lack of balance endearing rather than ungainly. And I wanted you so damned much I could hardly think straight! You were only eighteen years old, and too damned young for me, but I wanted you anyway. Fell in love with you anyway. Plus,' he continued firmly as she would have spoken, 'after your father was arrested and you refused all my attempts at trying to speak with you again, I also had every reason to believe you hated my guts.'

Bryn stared up at him dazedly, sure that she couldn't have heard him correctly. Gabriel couldn't really have just said— 'I never hated you, Gabriel.'

'Of course you did.'

'I hated the situation, not you,' she corrected. 'Would rather none of it had ever happened. But I know, I accept now, that my father was far from perfect, that he was responsible for what happened to him, no one else.' She looked up at him again. 'Gabriel, what did you do to help us five years ago?'

He grimaced. 'Do we really have to talk about that now?'

'Yes, we really do,' she insisted stubbornly.

He sighed. 'I'd rather not.'

'And I would rather you did.'

'You are so damned stubborn,' he sighed.

'Takes one to know one,' she came back ruefully. 'And if you don't tell me then I'll just ask my mother to tell me instead.'

Gabriel scowled his defeat as he sighed deeply. 'I—' He breathed deeply. 'I paid all your father's legal fees.'

Bryn just stared at him. All this time she had thought— Believed— 'What else...?' she breathed softly.

'Isn't that enough?' he drawled.

'What else, Gabriel?' she persisted.

His mouth thinned. 'I gave your mother enough money for the two of you to be able to move back to Wales. I wanted to give her more, enough to pay for you to go to university, but Mary wouldn't hear of it.'

'I should hope not!' Bryn was absolutely stunned at learning how Gabriel had helped them all those years ago. 'You really live up to your name, don't you?' she said wonderingly.

'Don't give me a false halo, Bryn,' Gabriel rasped harshly. 'I helped the two of you because someone had to.'

'And it had absolutely nothing to do with the fact that you had fallen in love with William Harper's overweight daughter?' she chided, an emotional catch in her throat for the man that Gabriel was, and always had been.

'Voluptuously sexy,' Gabriel insisted. 'Which is exactly how you'll look when you're pregnant with our child. You do want children, I hope?'

'Stop changing the subject.'

'Just thinking of you all round with our child,' he continued gruffly, 'with your breasts so big they spill over the top of your bra, is enough to make me hard.'

'Gabriel!' Bryn stood up abruptly, her breathing uneven as she realised what he had said, what his words implied. A baby? Gabriel was talking about the two of them having a child together?

He quirked a self-derisive brow. 'Too much honesty for you?'

Not enough. Not nearly enough!

She moistened her lips with the tip of her tongue, feeling a thrill run through her as she saw the way Gabriel's eyes instantly darkened at the provocation. 'I— When exactly do you intend us having this baby?'

'I think, for your mother and Rhys's sake, and my own parents', that we should probably wait until after we're married.'

'Married?' she squeaked.

'Married,' Gabriel confirmed decisively.

'But you wanted an affair.'

'You *assumed* I wanted an affair,' he corrected. 'When we met again four weeks ago and I obviously couldn't keep my hands off you, I decided to just take whatever you were willing to give me. But following on from your own honesty just now, you should know from the outset that I am very much in love with you, more so now even than five years ago, and that I won't settle for anything less than the two of us being married to each other.'

Happiness swelled so big and so wide inside her that Bryn felt as if she might actually explode from trying to contain it. Gabriel loved her. Had always loved her. He wanted to *marry* her. Have babies with her!

'I— You haven't asked me yet,' she reminded him breathlessly.

He grimaced. 'I've learned that asking sometimes isn't the right way to go about things where you're concerned.'

'Try me,' she encouraged huskily.

Gabriel looked searchingly into the glowing depths of her deep grey eyes, noting the flush in her cheeks, those slightly parted and oh-so-kissable lips. 'Will you marry me, Bryn?' he prompted huskily.

'Oh, yes, Gabriel. Yes, yes, yes!' She threw herself into his arms. 'Whenever and wherever you want.'

'As soon as it can be arranged.' His arms closed tightly about her.

'We've already wasted five years. I don't want to waste any more, want to spend the rest of my life telling you, showing you, how much I love you, will always love you!'

Bryn glowed with happiness as she imagined the future, a lifetime with Gabriel, years and years together, when they would show and tell each other how much they were loved.

* * * * *

A sneaky peek at next month...

MODERN™

POWER, PASSION AND IRRESISTIBLE TEMPTATION

My wish list for next month's titles...

In stores from 21st February 2014:

❑ A Prize Beyond Jewels — Carole Mortimer

❑ Pretender to the Throne — Maisey Yates

❑ The Sheikh's Last Seduction — Jennie Lucas

❑ The Woman Sent to Tame Him — Victoria Parker

In stores from 7th March 2014:

❑ A Queen for the Taking? — Kate Hewitt

❑ An Exception to His Rule — Lindsay Armstrong

❑ Enthralled by Moretti — Cathy Williams

❑ What a Sicilian Husband Wants — Michelle Smart

Available at WHSmith, Tesco, Asda, Eason, Amazon and Apple

Just can't wait?

Special Offers

Every month we put together collections and longer reads written by your favourite authors.

Here are some of next month's highlights— and don't miss our fabulous discount online!

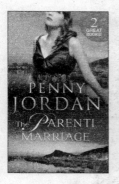

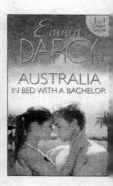

On sale 21st February   On sale 28th February   On sale 21st February

 **Save 20%** *on all Special Releases*

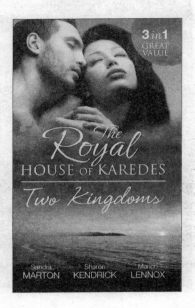

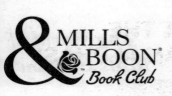

Join the Mills & Boon Book Club

Want to read more **Modern**™ books?
We're offering you **2 more** absolutely **FREE!**

We'll also treat you to these fabulous extras:

- Exclusive offers and much more!

- FREE home delivery

- FREE books and gifts with our special rewards scheme

Get your free books now!

visit www.millsandboon.co.uk/bookclub
or call Customer Relations on 020 8288 2888

Discover more romance at

www.millsandboon.co.uk

- 💜 WIN great prizes in our exclusive competitions

- 💜 BUY new titles before they hit the shops

- 💜 BROWSE new books and REVIEW your favourites

- 💜 SAVE on new books with the Mills & Boon® Bookclub™

- 💜 DISCOVER new authors

PLUS, to chat about your favourite reads, get the latest news and find special offers:

- 📘 Find us on facebook.com/millsandboon

- 🐦 Follow us on twitter.com/millsandboonuk

- 💜 Sign up to our newsletter at millsandboon.co.uk